ENDOR

"Lavo hooked me from the very beginning with a woman to root for, a romantic interest to swoon over, and an infuriating injustice to rail against. With compelling characters and rich description, Lavo puts the reader into the heart of a contemporary tale of lost-and-rediscovered love."

—Lori Z. Scott,
award-winning author of *Inside the Ten-Foot Line*

"Nancy Lavo is a fresh, exciting voice in Christian fiction. In *The Place Where You Belong*, book 1 in her Lone Star Loves series, she takes us to a small-town, all-up-in-your-business Texas community. With crisp, natural dialogue, she introduces diverse and quirky characters so relatable, you'll swear you've met them before in real life. As Hallie deals with her aging mother, the reader commiserates with her feelings of frustration playing tug-of-war with the love she bears. This compassionate and joyful novel reminds us how important it is to forgive and illustrates how God can empower us to do so, even when we don't think we can. You will laugh out loud as you cheer on Hallie and Trey. Lavo explores how an unexpected life change can be one's greatest blessing if we'll allow God to guide our steps. You're going to find this book hard to put down, and the glow you get from reading it will linger. Enjoy!"

—Paula Peckham,
award-winning author of the San Antonio series

"Nancy Lavo's writing has a good rhythm that grabs readers and keeps them turning the pages. I loved her well-developed main characters. They pulled me right into the story with them and didn't let me go until the end of the book. Some of her secondary characters helped accentuate the tensions between the main characters. Others paved the way for new understandings. Village Green is a wonderful setting for the story. I love a book with a satisfying ending, like the one in this novel."

—Lena Nelson Dooley,
author of the Love's Road Home series

LONE STAR LOVES

The Place Where You Belong

BOOK 1

NANCY LAVO

Birmingham, Alabama

The Place Where You Belong

Iron Stream Fiction
An imprint of Iron Stream Media
100 Missionary Ridge
Birmingham, AL 35242
IronStreamMedia.com

Library of Congress Control Number: 2022950024

Cover design by For the Muse Designs
ISBN: 978-1-56309-635-8 (paperback)
ISBN: 978-1-56309-636-5 (e-book)
1 2 3 4 5—27 26 25 24 23

DEDICATION

This book is dedicated to my Heavenly Father—the
lover of my soul, the source of my strength,
and the gracious giver of second chances.

ACKNOWLEDGMENTS

I'm grateful to Lena Nelson Dooley and the members of her critique group for their teaching and encouragement.

I'm grateful to Tamela Hancock Murray for her wise representation.

I'm grateful to Larry Leech and the team at Iron Stream Media for their editorial insight and hard work to make my book the very best it can be.

Finally, I'm grateful to my husband and family for their love and unwavering support.

CHAPTER ONE

H allie Nichols hated to go home.

Every mile closer raised her level of tension. She tightened her grip on the steering wheel and blew out a breath.

I can do this.

Three days—a week, tops—and I'll be out of here.

She injected an extra dose of determined optimism into her voice while repeating the declaration to her reflection in the rearview mirror.

"I can do this."

Open fields lush with new spring growth slid by the window as she reached across to the bag on her passenger seat and pulled out one of her ever-ready rolls of antacids. She thumbed off a couple and chewed them up to extinguish the burn in the pit of her stomach.

Her temples continued to pound despite the Tylenol she'd taken earlier. No point in taking any more. Beyond the potential damage to her liver, she knew there wasn't enough painkiller in the great state of Texas to cure her "homecoming blues."

A reluctant grin pulled at the corner of her mouth. If only she had the talent to set her current outlook to music, she'd have the makings of a best-selling country song.

She slowed her car when the faded green sign marking the city limits came into view. A tangle of thorny brown vines crept up the rusted post and across the face of the sign, nearly choking off the words: Village Green, Population 571. She released a long, noisy sigh.

Welcome home.

She hung a left off the two-lane highway at the flashing yellow light, heading south on Main Street. Though hers was the only car on the road, she eased off the gas, slowing to twenty miles an hour to stall for time. She tightened her grip on the steering wheel. And sighed.

Rolling along at a crawl gave her the opportunity to study the weathered brick storefronts lining the street. In the glare of March sunlight, everything looked tired and dirty. At least half of the old two-story buildings were boarded up. Since its heyday in the fifties, the sleepy town of Village Green was slowly dwindling away.

Hallie flicked her fingers in a dismissive wave. Good riddance. She couldn't muster a single sentimental twinge for the town where she'd been born and raised. Village Green was nothing more than a jumble of stinging slights and painful memories.

She edged past an unfamiliar pickup truck parked in front of her childhood home and pulled into the rutted gravel driveway. She shifted into Park and looked through the windshield to see her all-time worst memory sitting next to her mom on the porch swing.

Trey Gunther.

Hallie resisted the very real temptation to slam her car into Reverse, squeal out of the driveway in a spray of stones, and beat a fast path back to the city.

Once a fixture at Hallie's house, she swore Trey hadn't stepped foot on the Nichols's property in a decade. After their less-than-amicable breakup, they'd made it a point to steer clear of each other. Since they hadn't shared more than a curt nod or two in the last ten years, she couldn't imagine what brought him today.

She squinted for another look. Definitely Trey. No mistaking his broad shoulders and sun-streaked hair.

Hallie took her time switching off the ignition, giving herself a minute to assimilate this unexpected twist. Curiosity warred with homecoming dread.

What was he doing here?

She climbed out of the car and pocketed the keys without locking up, leaving everything to unload later. Several thoughts raced through her mind as she pushed her door closed. What had she done to deserve having her old boyfriend on her reception committee? Why couldn't she have worn something classier than her oldest pair of jeans and a T-shirt she should have thrown out years ago?

And most importantly, how should she act toward him?

She couldn't very well ignore him since he was sitting there, big as life. And she had no intention of running up the white flag and making friendly with the man who had broken her heart. So what did that leave her?

She caught her bottom lip in her teeth. Think, Hallie. Creating images was her stock-in-trade, right? If she could make a living teaching people how to appear cool and unflappable, she should be able to pull off the same thing for herself. She took a deep breath, releasing it slowly. *Come on, girl, you can do it.*

She'd been over him a long time. She may be shaken by his surprise appearance, but truthfully, Trey Gunther no longer rated even a minor blip on her radar.

Hallie crossed the small square of freshly mown lawn. From the cover of her sunglasses, she made a quick survey of her welcoming committee, now standing at the top of the stairs.

Her mom looked tired. Poor thing. She'd aged a lot in the month since her stroke. Once a bundle of energy, the stroke had broken her. The board-straight posture she'd modeled for her two daughters had been replaced with stooped shoulders and a wobbly stance. She'd lost weight in rehab, even more in the few days since Hallie had last seen her. This morning her peach-colored track suit hung loosely on her hunched frame. Standing beside Trey, she looked positively fragile.

Hallie's gaze shifted. Trey looked fabulous. Darn it. It'd be a whole lot easier to play it cool if his hair had decided to recede and his waistline expanded.

Funny, she thought as she closed the distance between them, she'd forgotten just how good-looking Trey was. Of course, she hadn't been within twenty feet of him in close to a decade. Evidently, she'd let bitterness distort her memories. Over time she'd half-convinced herself he was just an average-looking guy.

Tall and tan with thick, blond-streaked hair and a chiseled face with three-day-old whiskers that brought out a handsome ruggedness, he could be a poster boy for Mr. All-American Hunk. Beyond being blessed with great looks, Trey had always possessed an indefinable something that drew people to him like a magnet drew metal. Even as a teenager, Trey had exuded charm by the truckload. The rock-solid presence of him seemed to promise stability. People immediately assumed Trey was dependable and trustworthy.

Which just went to show how wrong assumptions could be.

"Hallie!" Her mother lifted her four-pronged cane in a jerky wave, her left arm dangling at her side like a broken wing.

Ignoring him for the moment, Hallie trotted up the painted wooden steps and gathered her mother into a gentle hug, careful not to upset her precarious balance. "Hi, Mom. How are you feeling?"

"Better now that I'm home." Her mother drew back, a fresh coat of her trademark tangerine lipstick on her smile. "Aren't you surprised to see Trey here?"

Though surprise didn't begin to cover her feelings at seeing her old flame standing on her porch, she kept her expression neutral when she turned toward him. "Hey."

"Hey." His smile was as impersonal as hers, his gaze cool and assessing. He must have felt his presence required an explanation. "My mom planned to drive your mother this morning, but her arthritis was acting up, so I offered to bring your mother home."

Hallie didn't know where the tiny dart of disappointment came from. She hadn't honestly believed he was here to confess he'd suddenly discovered he couldn't live another minute without her. Even so, she'd be lying to say she hadn't fantasized a time or two about Trey crawling to her one day, begging her to take him back. The highlight of the fantasy was the pleasure of rejecting him, just as he'd rejected her.

She should have known it was a good neighbor thing that brought him to her mother's porch. Village Green was all about good neighbors. The Gunther family was all about Village Green. And Trey was the consummate Gunther.

Hallie nodded. "Thanks."

"Come on in the house, you two." Her mother appeared unaware of any emotional undercurrents. "I'm exhausted from standing here."

Hallie pulled open the screen door and stepped aside for her mother to enter. She followed close behind, her hand poised at the small of the older woman's back in case she should stumble. The stroke had affected the left side of her body, so her mom was learning to walk again. No longer reflexive, each step required deliberate thought and placement of her feet and cane. It felt like an eternity just to walk a few feet inside the door.

Her mother was winded by the time Hallie escorted her to her favorite armchair by the window. She collapsed into the seat, sighing with pleasure while she settled in.

The sound tugged at Hallie's heartstrings. She'd been so caught up in her own misery, she'd almost lost sight of who had truly suffered through all of this. Sure, she'd been inconvenienced and dragged back to the black hole of Village Green, but only temporarily. Her mother's life had been radically altered forever. Physically, mentally, emotionally. She'd need months of therapy to regain even a fraction of all she had lost. And between her stay at the hospital and the one at the rehab center, she'd been gone from her beloved home for nearly six weeks.

"I think there are still some sodas in the fridge," her mother said after she caught her breath. "Why don't you get us all something cold to drink?"

Hallie glanced at Trey and lifted a brow. This was his opportunity to escape. He'd done his good deed and upheld the family honor. No point in him hanging around and making her uncomfortable.

He didn't move.

Maybe he needed a nudge. "I'm sure Trey has things to do."

She waited for his polite excuse. Instead, he smiled at her mother and nodded. "Something to drink sounds great."

Hallie frowned. Apparently, the Gunther notion of neighborliness included chitchat over refreshments. Just what she didn't need. He could be here for hours.

She tried to find a bright spot in her increasingly dismal morning. Her head still ached, and the antacids hadn't touched the fire in her stomach. The only positive she could see was if she was stuck with Trey, at least he'd have to shoulder part of the burden of making conversation with her mother.

Guilt welled, tightening in her chest. She had tried, *really* tried, to build a friendship with her mom. As a child, she'd worked endlessly to earn her mother's affection. As an adult, she'd made the calls, sent the emails, issued the invitations. But they'd never really connected. It wasn't that her mother didn't love her. It was just that Hallie would never be Janice.

"Cold drinks coming up." Hallie headed down the short hall to the kitchen and switched on the overhead light. The familiarity of her old home hit her hard. The beige linoleum in the faux pebble pattern, the ruffled valance hanging over the window at the sink, the dark wood dinette her father had surprised her mother with on their anniversary—all unchanged. Even the smells were those she remembered from childhood.

She grabbed a couple sodas from the refrigerator. After filling three tall glasses with ice and cola, she scooped them up and carried them back to the living room.

She extended a glass to Trey, carefully avoiding his eyes and his touch before placing her own drink on the corner of the coffee table, positioning herself as far from him as possible without moving to another room. Hallie brought the third glass to her mother, transferring it slowly to make certain she had a good grip. "Got it?"

Her mom nodded. "Yes, thank you. Before you sit down, will you run and get me a towel to put on my lap in case I spill?"

Because her coordination was off, spills were a big part of her mom's new reality. Hallie hurried to the bathroom, pulled a clean, pink-striped hand towel off the bar, and headed back. "Do you want me to pin it around your neck?"

"No, just prop it under my chin." She lifted her face, waiting while Hallie leaned over her and tucked it into her collar.

The towel smoothed to her mother's satisfaction, Hallie took a seat on the chair beside her. Even though she'd been doing her best to ignore him, she'd been painfully aware of Trey watching the interaction between her and her mom.

"It's obvious Hallie will have you spoiled in no time," he said.

Her mother smiled and nodded. "She's been a fine help. Speaking of help, have either of you heard from Janice today?"

Both Hallie and Trey shook their heads.

"I expected her to call this morning." Her mother's forehead knotted, and she glanced toward the phone on the end table. "I hope everything is all right."

"I'm sure she's fine, Mom."

Trey nodded reassuringly.

"She wasn't able to visit me at the rehab center. Not that I expected it." Her expression softened into the doting look reserved for discussions of her eldest daughter. "We all know how busy she is. She did telephone me several times. Such a thoughtful girl. With all her responsibilities to her husband and the college, she still finds the time to check on her mother. I'm certain she'll come now that I'm home." She glanced at Hallie and sighed heavily. "I don't know how we'll manage till she gets here."

Hallie nodded, her smile never faltering though her heart did a sad little slide. Like a dutiful daughter, she'd dropped everything to come home and care for her mom. But her mother didn't want her. She wanted Janice.

Hallie wasn't a stupid woman. She didn't know why she'd dared to hope this time would be different. The fact was, it didn't matter how much time passed, some things never changed. Regardless of what she did, no matter how hard she tried, she just didn't measure up to her older sister.

Trey and her mom carried the conversation for thirty minutes or so while they finished their drinks, but Hallie contributed little to the small talk. Back less than an hour and she was already sinking under a churning tide of insecurity. It seemed all she had to do was drive inside the city limits and suddenly everything she'd accomplished faded to nothing—the public relations company she'd built with her own hands, the good friends who believed in her, the nice bank account. All forgotten. Here she was nothing more than Mrs. Nichols's other daughter, Janice's insignificant little sister.

She'd promised herself she wouldn't let it happen again, but despite her best intentions, this town, this house, these people managed to whittle her down to nothing.

Too restless to sit, Hallie popped up from her chair. "I think I'll go out and get my stuff from the car."

Trey stood as well. "I'll help you."

She gave him a bland smile. "No, thanks." That's just what she needed. A life-sized reminder that everyone preferred Janice.

"Of course she wants your help," her mother said. "Hallie, let Trey carry the heavy stuff. We might as well make use of all those muscles while they are handy." She chuckled.

Because arguing would make her look as stupid as she'd begun to feel, Hallie accepted with a shrug. "Okay, great."

She and Trey walked to her car in awkward silence, two semi-hostile strangers who'd once pledged to love one another forever. She dug the keys from the pocket of her jeans and opened the trunk.

"Your mom seems good." Trey pulled out her two large suitcases. "It's really lucky about the stroke."

Though she'd been careful to avoid making eye contact with him all morning, she glared at him now. "Lucky?"

Lucky she'd spent a week sleeping on the cramped fold-out chair in her mother's hospital room, worried sick about the future? Lucky she'd been burning up the highway between Fort Worth and Corsicana for the last month so she could spend every weekend with her mom in rehab? Lucky she'd been dragged back to Village Green to have the life sapped out of her?

One look at her face had him lifting his palms in surrender. "Let me rephrase that. What I meant to say is it's lucky the stroke wasn't more severe. That it didn't affect her thinking or her speech."

Her spike of temper cooled. "I don't know if I'd go so far as to say we're lucky, but I guess it could be a lot worse." She pulled her tote from the trunk and slung it over her shoulder, carrying her laptop case in her other hand. She followed Trey up the stairs, stifling a sigh when the muscles in his powerful arms bulged with the weight of her luggage.

Whatever else she could say about Trey, there was no denying he was a fine specimen of a man. Since there was no rule that she had to *like* him to admire his physique, she allowed herself a moment to appreciate it.

He'd had a great build in high school—a swoon-worthy ratio of height to muscle—and from the look of things, he'd only improved with age. Hallie remembered hearing her mother mention Trey served as cocaptain of the town's softball team. Seemed the game was doing a pretty fine job of keeping things bronzed and toned.

He lugged her bags through the front door. "Mrs. Nichols, do you want me to put Hallie in Janice's room since it's closer to yours?"

She shook her head. "No, you'd better not. Janice will want her own room when she gets here."

Trey shrugged at Hallie who waited behind him. She returned the shrug then tipped up her chin, directing him down the hall to her old room.

Hallie had shared a bedroom with her sister, across the hall from her parents, until Janice turned thirteen and decided she needed a room of her own. To keep the peace, Hallie's dad had converted the small room off the kitchen into a bedroom for Hallie.

The narrow, rectangular room had been just the right size for a ten-year-old.

She could still remember her excitement on the trip to the Penney's catalog store to furnish her new space. She'd fallen hard for the white-and-gold French provincial set. Eighteen years later the twin bed, chest of drawers, and desk still snugged nicely into her old room.

Trey flicked on the overhead light and squeezed his eyes shut in an exaggerated grimace. "Man! I don't know how you slept in a room this pink."

Hallie glanced around the tiny room. "Are you kidding? It's a great color."

Her first choice had been lavender, the soft powdery purple of a spring lilac. The trouble was Janice had been pretty taken with the paint chips her father had brought home to Hallie from the hardware store and decided *she* wanted the lavender on her walls. Being older, and being Janice, she got the lavender. And as Hallie had been warned not to copy her older sister, she'd settled for pink.

She crossed to the desk and set her computer bag on top. "Just put the suitcases on the bed, please. I'll unpack later."

He hefted them up, laying them side by side on the pink gingham spread. They turned at the same time, coming face-to-face, inches apart in the tiny room. Hallie froze. He was so close she could feel the warmth of his breath on her cheek, the cool weight of his gaze as he studied her.

She'd once compared his honey-gold eyes to those of a lion. This morning she was struck again by the similarity. Beneath strong brows and spiky lashes, his eyes gleamed with intelligence, confidence, and strength. Like his jungle counterpart, Trey was easy with his power and position.

His gaze traveled slowly over her face. Analyzing. Measuring. Like he was trying to see inside of her, to her deepest thoughts. Though tempted to lower her eyes and break the unnerving connection, she held her ground. She wouldn't give him the satisfaction of seeing her squirm.

After a long moment of silent scrutiny, Trey blinked. "If you don't need anything, I'll be running along. I want to get into the bank this morning."

Hallie nodded. Her inclination was to let him find his own way out, but ingrained good manners and the fact he'd been so nice to her mother had her walking him to the door.

"Thanks for everything, Trey," her mom called from her chair. "Please tell your mother I hope she gets to feeling better."

"Yes, ma'am, I will. And you take care." With a quick jerk of his head, he motioned for Hallie to step out onto the porch with him. After pushing the door closed behind them, he turned to her and lowered his voice. "Are you two going to be all right?"

Hallie nodded. "We'll be fine."

"If you need anything—"

She resisted rolling her eyes. It had been a long time since she needed anything from him. "We've got it covered."

"Okay." Standing there, hands shoved into his pockets and the sunlight glinting off his golden head, he didn't look much different from the eighteen-year-old she'd loved so completely. The kid who'd held her heart and her trust and had cruelly crushed them both.

He started across the porch toward the stairs, paused, and turned to face her. "It may not show, but I know your mother appreciates you and the sacrifices you've made. She's really thankful you've come home to take care of her."

It felt so nice to think her mother valued her. Warmed by his words, Hallie opened her mouth to thank him when the implication of what he'd said sank in. She frowned. "Wait a minute. You don't think I'm staying?"

He lifted his broad shoulders. "Sure. It's obvious your mother is in no shape to live independently."

"Yeah, but—"

His expression turned wry. "You don't honestly think Janice is coming home to take care of her, do you?"

Hallie snorted. "Hardly. But I only came back to make arrangements for Mom's care. I'm not moving to Village Green."

She lifted a hand to stop the protest she saw on his lips. "I know living here is the sum total of your aspirations, but it's not mine. I've got a great life back in Fort Worth. No way I'm giving it up." She lowered her voice. "I could never come back here."

Embarrassed she'd shown more emotion than she'd intended, Hallie cleared her throat. "I'm here to make the arrangements for my mom, then I'm gone."

"So much for trying to help out." Trey climbed into his truck and fired up the engine. It seemed ten years wasn't long enough for Hallie to work through her hostility issues. He shrugged before shifting into Drive and cruising down the block.

Her problem, not his.

When he'd agreed to pick up Mrs. Nichols from the rehab center, he'd hadn't given much thought to the fact he'd see Hallie. Not that seeing her would have changed anything. Doing favors for neighbors and acting as a helping hand in the community had been bred into Trey as it had for generations of Gunthers.

His family had been principal players in Village Green since its formation. He was proud of his heritage, proud to be a part of the people who had served as leaders in the small town for the last hundred years. If the Gunthers had a family crest, the motto at the bottom would read, "With privilege comes responsibility." *Noblesse oblige.*

The wheels of change moved slowly in small towns. People still came to Trey or his father looking for advice or help. The fact that the Gunthers controlled the bank ensured their prominence in the future.

Though he might not agree with the small-town mentality, Trey understood it. He respected it. And did his part to uphold it.

Picking up Mrs. Nichols was no problem. Besides being her banker, he considered himself her friend.

And Hallie posed no problem either. She was ancient history, a mistake he'd long forgotten. After ten years, he was totally over her.

Which was not to say he wasn't curious.

Curiosity had him waiting on the porch beside Mrs. Nichols for Hallie's arrival. What were her plans now that her mother was incapacitated? Would she move back to Village Green? Did he want that? And okay, he could admit it, he'd wondered if he would find some sign she'd finally realized that giving him up was the biggest mistake of her life. Not that he'd believed she'd been pining away for him for the last ten years, but she'd dealt his pride a major blow, and it would have been satisfying to know she'd suffered a little.

No such luck.

Hallie didn't look regretful. She looked cool and confident. She didn't look like she was suffering. She looked like a million bucks.

Hallie had always been a beauty in a quiet, take-a-second-look sort of way. Nothing quiet about her now.

She'd changed her hairstyle since last he'd seen her. She'd replaced the long, thick mane she'd always worn with choppy shoulder-length waves. The new style had big city written all over it in a flirty, self-confident sort of way. Curiosity made his fingers itch to reach out and touch it, to see if it was as soft and silky as he'd remembered. Wisdom had him keeping his hands to himself.

He'd always thought her eyes were her best feature. Big and brown and luminous, she used to melt his heart with a look.

He'd watched those expressive eyes fill with hurt this morning when her mother spoke about Janice taking care of things. Trey reminded himself the look in Hallie's eyes was no longer his responsibility.

Her parents never made a secret of their preference for their eldest daughter. As a teen, the blatant favoritism had made him furious. Anyone with an ounce of intelligence could see quiet Hallie was worth a dozen flashy Janices.

Again, not his problem.

Now they'd had their first meeting, and his curiosity was satisfied.

Hallie might look different, but she hadn't changed. History had repeated itself on her porch just now when she rejected his help. And his town.

No, Hallie hadn't changed.

But then, neither had he.

Gunther men didn't back down.

And Gunther men didn't beg.

CHAPTER TWO

Hallie unpacked while her mother napped. She'd brought an impressive selection of clothing for her short stay, as she was depending on her clothes to project the confidence she never felt here at home. Still, it took less than half an hour to get everything tucked away into the closet and drawers. Finished, she sat on her bed, slumping back against the mound of lacy pillows with a sigh of satisfaction.

Trey was right about one thing. The room was extremely pink. But rather than oppressive, it seemed hopeful. It was a happy, vibrant pink that captured the essence of a young girl edging toward womanhood.

She smiled. She'd woven her share of dreams in this tiny box of a room over the years. Dreams of the straight teeth she'd have when the hated braces finally came off, of developing curves to round out her coltish body, of making a name for herself in the world.

Her dreams had been full of the handsome prince who would love her through eternity. Tall, blonde, and handsome enough to make her chest ache, Trey Gunther had been her ideal for as long as she could remember. He was the prince who would love her for all time.

She picked up a small round pillow edged in worn white lace and hugged it to her chest. As far as dreams went, she'd done pretty well. The braces had finally come off, revealing a straight-toothed smile, curves had appeared in all the right places, and she was building a name for herself with the small public relations company she'd started in Fort Worth.

She didn't end up with the prince, but that was okay. He turned out to be a toad anyway. She was much better off without him.

When her thoughts took a dangerous detour back to Trey for the zillionth time since he'd driven away, Hallie hopped off the bed to find something to do. She'd spent years purging him from her heart and head. No way she'd let a chance meeting undo all her hard work.

She trotted into the kitchen for a nice carb-loaded snack to take her mind off he-who-would-no-longer-be-mentioned. She swung open the refrigerator door and peeked inside to make her selection. Other than a couple cans of cola and the usual assortment of condiments, the refrigerator was pretty much empty. A neighbor must have come in and cleaned it out, knowing her mother wouldn't be home for a month.

Sighing, Hallie closed the door. If they didn't want to starve, she'd have to make a run to the grocery store. This visit was shaping up to be a real nightmare.

Back only a couple of hours and she'd spent close to a third of it with the man she'd sworn to forget. Now she would have to go into town and face down the old ghosts who resurrected every time she saw a familiar face.

Village Green was crammed with memories she wanted to erase. The thousand hurtful little digs and slights she'd endured growing up, the lopsided comparisons to Janice, the well-meaning remarks urging her to exert herself so maybe she could be as pretty and popular as her sister.

In the years since she'd moved away, Hallie had developed a system to combat the memories. Even after her father died, she kept her visits short and confined herself to her parents' house.

She'd known from the start this visit would be different. She'd anticipated that as her mother's caretaker she couldn't hide. Out of necessity Hallie would have to run errands and accompany her mom. But she never dreamed she'd be forced to spend time with Trey.

Hallie's resolve firmed. She was committed to arranging for her mom's care. Until then, she had no choice but to grit her teeth and face down the past. On one point, however, she would not budge. She refused to spend even one more minute in the company of Trey Gunther.

She looked up at the sound of a cane thumping along the wooden floor in the hall. "Nap over already?"

"I couldn't sleep." Her mom stopped in the kitchen doorway. Her graying hair stood in unruly tufts, reminding Hallie she had missed her last salon appointment. "Too much on my mind, I guess. Did you call your sister?"

"Yes, ma'am. She didn't answer, so I left her a voice mail."

Her mother's face fell into disappointed creases. "Oh. Did you tell her to call me?"

"Yup." Hallie crossed the room and rubbed a hand along her mother's back. "Don't worry. She'll call when she gets the message." She chose not to mention she doubted her sister would make returning the call a priority.

"I hope she hurries." Tears filled her mother's eyes, and her voice wobbled. "I just don't know how we'll manage."

Another razor-sharp reminder that although Hallie was here, doing her best, it wasn't enough. She wasn't enough.

"I made you a grocery list." Her mother handed her a half sheet of paper covered with wobbly script. "We don't have a thing to eat in the house."

"No problem." Hallie tucked the hurt and the list away. "I'll run up to the store."

"Good. And while you're out, you'll need to stop by the bank and get my checkbook from Trey."

Hallie frowned. "Why in the world would Trey have your checkbook?"

Her mom shrugged. "I guess it's because that's the arrangement we made."

Half an hour later, Hallie whipped her car into one of the diagonal parking spaces on the street in front of the bank. She shut off the ignition and slammed out of the car, pausing momentarily to smooth her black power skirt, then stomped into the bank to do a little "un-arranging."

Walking through the heavy doors of the Village Green Bank and Trust was like passing through a time warp. Unlike the modern sterility of her bank in Fort Worth, the B&T resembled a quaint Victorian parlor. The carved paneling on the walls gleamed beneath antique brass lamps. Sofas of rich tobacco leather and polished wood tables were positioned around the small lobby to encourage patrons to sit and visit. Hallie knew a buffet was set out each morning with coffee and fresh muffins.

She refused to be charmed by the homey ambiance. She was a woman on a mission.

How dare Trey meddle in her family's affairs? He had no right. If he was operating under the mistaken assumption they welcomed his interference, she was about to set him straight. They did not want or need anything from him.

"Hallie Nichols? Is that you?" Doug Swinton called from behind a wood-framed teller's window that belonged in another era. "It's great to see you."

Because he'd been a dear friend of her father's, Hallie slowed to speak to him. "Hi, Mr. Swinton. How have you been?"

"Can't complain." He pushed his wire-framed glasses higher on his nose. "Listen, I'm awfully sorry to hear about your mother. I know this is a hard time for your family."

She smiled. "Thank you."

"I expect your sister will be coming home to take care of everything?"

Instead of going with her first impulse to assure him she was more than capable of caring for her mother, Hallie said, "We haven't firmed up our plans yet."

He nodded. "Please let me know if there's anything we can do for you. I know my Kay is eager to bring supper over to you."

It was impossible to take offense in the face of his genuine concern. "That would be great. Have Miss Kay give me a call at Mom's house, and we'll work something out."

"Will do. You tell your mother hello for me."

"Yes, sir. Good to see you." She waved as she hurried off in the direction of the bank offices, determined not to be waylaid again.

Old Miss Tillie, a fixture at the bank since Moses was delivering the tablets, sat at the reception desk for the executive offices. She stood when Hallie approached. "Well, lookee here. Little Hallie Nichols, as I live and breathe."

"Yes, ma'am, it's me." Hallie moved into Miss Tillie's outstretched arms for the proffered hug.

After a quick embrace, Miss Tillie clamped surprisingly strong, age-spotted hands on Hallie's arms and scooted her back a step to take a better look. "Aren't you looking just fine?" After a prolonged study, she gave an approving nod. "You've cut your hair, haven't you? Real stylish."

"Thank you." Hallie felt her cheeks heat under the scrutiny. "I need to see Trey. Is he in?"

Miss Tillie pinned her with a sharp look from beneath darkly penciled brows. "Is there a problem?"

Hallie shook her head. Privacy did not exist in Village Green, so she might as well answer the prying questions. "No, ma'am. I just came to get my mom's checkbook."

The woman nodded. "That's right, he handles your mother's money now, doesn't he? Tell me, how is your poor mother?"

"She's better, thank you."

"A stroke is a terrible thing," Tillie said with a mournful wag. "And her being so young. I know you must be at your wits end wondering what to do. When's Janice coming home?"

Hallie felt the muscles in her face tighten. "I'm not sure."

"Well, don't you worry." Miss Tillie patted Hallie's arm. "She'll be home before you know it, and everything will be just fine."

Apparently, there wasn't a soul in Village Green who thought Hallie could do the job. She glanced beyond Miss Tillie's slight shoulders to the doors of the executive offices. "I hate to rush you, but I need to get in to see Trey as soon as possible. I worry about leaving Mom alone too long."

"You're absolutely right." She took two steps toward the offices, stopped, and narrowed her eyes at Hallie. "Don't I remember something about you and Trey being an item?" She pressed a fingertip to her bright red lips, brows furrowed as if she were delving into the recesses of her memory. "Yes, I'm sure of it. You two were high school sweethearts, weren't you?"

In what she knew would be the first of many times in her short stay, Hallie batted the ghost away with an easy flick of her wrist. "Old news, Miss Tillie. Nothing but old news."

After one last appraising look, Miss Tillie walked Hallie to Trey's door, another example of finely carved mahogany, this with a discreet brass plate engraved with Trey's name. She knocked once before pushing it open without waiting for a response. "Mr. Gunther, your old friend Hallie Nichols is here to see you."

Trey glanced up from his computer screen, his eyes wide with surprise. Hallie noticed he'd pulled a navy sports coat over the polo shirt he'd been wearing earlier that morning. Her head of steam slipped a notch at the sight of him. Really, the man was too good-looking for his own good.

He stood and rounded the massive wooden desk to greet her. "Come in, Hallie." His smile was wary. "What can I do for you?"

The reminder of her mission helped Hallie refocus. She watched Miss Tillie toddle out and close the door behind her before hissing, "You can tell me why you've got my mother's checkbook."

His expression impassive, he motioned her to one of the two seats in front of his desk before returning to his high-backed, black leather chair. With maddening calm, he waited until he'd settled in, elbows propped on the arm rests, bronzed fingers steepled in front of him before answering. "Simple. Your family asked me to."

Hallie perched on the edge of her seat, nearly vibrating with anger. "That's funny. Seems like I would remember making a request like that."

His eyes crinkled at the corners. He had the nerve to smile as though it *was* funny. "You probably don't remember because you didn't make the request. Your sister did."

"My sister . . ." Hallie sputtered to a halt. "What does Janice have to do with this?"

"Everything. At least she does according to your father. In his will he stipulated that if anything happened to him and your mother, Janice, being the oldest, would handle any family business matters that arose. When your mother first had her stroke and there was some question as to her mental competency, I contacted Janice."

"But—"

He lifted a hand for silence. "I acted according to your father's instructions. I asked Janice how she wanted to proceed. She thought it would be a good idea for me to handle your mother's finances until such time that your mother is able to handle them for herself."

Hallie slumped back against her chair. All the fight whooshed out of her in one long frustrated breath. She could hardly blast him with the pithy speech she'd rehearsed on the drive over. He had the nerve to interfere because her sister asked him to.

He leaned forward, his expression cool. "Don't get the wrong idea. I didn't arrange this so I could insinuate myself into your good graces. This is not about you. Your mother is a client and a friend. I did it for her. I advised Janice to let me handle things. Under the circumstances, I think she made the best decision."

Hallie's spine stiffened. Did this man's ego have no end? Did he honestly think she hoped the two of them had a future? "I never thought it was about me. If you want to know the truth, I thought it was about the Gunther predilection for nosing into other people's business. It's no secret your family likes to flex its considerable muscle in the lives of others."

When Trey's brows shot up, she realized she'd let anger and frustration push her too far. A smart woman didn't antagonize the person holding all the cards.

She cleared her throat and forced a smile. "Regardless, I appreciate you looking out for my mother." She congratulated herself on her remarkably civilized tone. "So, how do we proceed from here?"

His gaze locked on hers. "I give you the checkbook, and you take care of what needs to be done."

"Really?" Excellent. The situation wasn't nearly as bad as she'd thought. She'd have him out of her hair in no time. Hallie felt the pressure in her chest ease and the beginning of a genuine smile turn up the corners of her mouth. "It's that easy? I don't have to clear it with you before I write a check?"

Trey studied her face for a long uncomfortable moment, then shook his head. "No. That would be insulting. As Miss Tillie said, we're old friends. I know you're more than capable of handling your mother's finances."

"Thank you." Shame for all the abuse she'd heaped on his head on the drive over and relief that she wouldn't have to spend another moment in his company had her adding real warmth to the smile she sent him. She stood and approached his desk. "I know you're busy. If you'll give me her checkbook, I'll let you get back to work."

He slid open his desk drawer and pulled out a checkbook with the worn, green plastic cover she recognized as her mother's. He handed it across the desk to her, but when she reached for it, his long-fingered grip tightened.

Hallie lifted her brows in question.

Trey waited until her gaze traveled from the checkbook up to meet his. "Why don't you plan to come in once a week, and we'll go over your expenditures."

Hallie's hand fell away empty. Her jaw went slack. "You're kidding, right? I'm sure I just heard you say I was capable of handling my mother's finances."

"Absolutely. But although I have complete faith in you, I promised your father and sister I'd manage the account." He flashed a wide smile of perfect white teeth that reminded Hallie of a lion, toying with its prey. "Think of this as a compromise. By meeting with me once a week you have the freedom to do as you see fit, and I'm keeping my word to your family." His chin firmed. "There is really no other option."

Hallie stared at him, dumbfounded. *This can't be happening.*

He tipped up a brow. "Is there a problem?"

She compressed her lips against the words waiting to spill out. *The problem is you. I don't want to meet with you. I don't want to talk to you. I don't want to see you. Ever.*

"Nothing I can't manage," she choked out. She snatched the checkbook from his now-loosened grip. "Thank you. I'll see you next week."

"Or sooner," Trey said under his breath as Hallie turned on her high heels and huffed out of his office, closing the door behind her with a sharp crack.

He eased back in his chair, elbows propped, fingertips touching. A slow grin stretched the corners of his mouth.

His old friend Hallie Nichols was mad.

Interesting. He was surprised to find so much heat beneath her very cool exterior.

He shouldn't have done it. He shouldn't have pushed her so far. But in all honesty, she started it. He'd been minding his own business when she marched into his office in her high heels and fancy black skirt. She looked so good he'd about had palpitations.

His mind temporarily befuddled by the sight of her, he figured his best strategy was to get behind the ancestral desk and into banker mode. By the time he'd made a dignified retreat to his chair, Hallie had worked herself into a chest-heaving tizzy, causing his blood pressure to ratchet up another notch or two.

His temper climbed with his blood pressure. She was getting to him, and that made him mad.

She'd made a fool of him once. She'd taken his love and thrown it back in his face. He'd worked hard to put that behind him. She did not have the power to tie him into knots anymore.

His blood was already on a low boil when she hit him with the remark about the Gunther family flexing their muscle in other people's lives. If the skirt and heels had been a blow to his solar plexus, then the dig about his family was a direct hit below the belt. And she knew it.

Still, he'd been able to retain his cool. He was a professional. He'd had a lot of years to come to terms with Hallie's rejection of him and the town his family built. But when her face lit up like a kid on Christmas morning after he'd told her she didn't have to check in with him, he'd lost it.

He'd foolishly believed she'd stormed into his office because she resented having someone look over her undoubtedly competent shoulders. He could understand that. But he'd read the situation wrong. The problem wasn't the fact her ex-boyfriend was handling her mother's money. It was the prospect of meeting with him that made her mad.

She honestly believed spending time with him would be torture.

The realization she thought of him as some sort of monster pushed him over the top. Where did she get off treating him like he was the plague? Had she forgotten *she'd* dumped *him*? That he was the good guy?

The more he thought about it, the madder he got. She thought he was a monster? Fine. He'd show her a monster.

He'd have no trouble flexing a little Gunther muscle and make her report to him once a week. He knew he shouldn't have done it. It was petty and unprofessional.

And it felt great.

It had been pure pleasure to watch her big brown eyes when she realized he was serious about meeting with him. He'd enjoyed watching the heat build on her expressive face so much that he'd hardly noticed her chest had begun to heave again.

Hardly.

And when she twitched out of his office, eyes flashing and color high—well, it just didn't get any better than that.

He'd suffered plenty. Now her turn.

Hallie probably wouldn't believe it, but his decision to handle her mother's finances was purely altruistic. Mrs. Nichols needed help. Trey was in a position to give it. Hallie had been out of the picture so long, he never dreamed she'd become involved.

It hadn't been difficult to talk Janice into letting him hold the financial reins. One phone call, a few compliments, and she was all for giving the job to him. His offer had given her an honorable release from an unpleasant task and given Trey the peace of mind knowing the funds would be there when Mrs. Nichols needed them.

He was surprised when Mrs. Nichols told him that Hallie would be returning to take care of her. She'd made it sound as though Hallie was coming home for good.

Wrong.

This morning's conversation on the porch cleared up that little misconception. Whatever was eating at Hallie, whatever had soured her on Village Green, was obviously still an issue. She'd sounded every bit as adamant today as she had ten years ago when out of the blue, she'd informed him that she wasn't sticking around his miserable one-horse town.

She'd made good on her threat. Other than occasional holiday visits to her folks, she hadn't been back.

Contrary to what she'd said this morning, staying in Village Green hadn't been Trey's sole ambition. He'd never told anyone, but like Hallie, he'd been eager to go someplace new, to try out his wings. As much as he loved Village Green, he'd wanted to make his own way in the world, to forge his own path in life.

Unlike Hallie, he didn't have that freedom.

Trey glanced over at the framed series of old black and white photographs covering his wall. Beginning with his great, great grandfather, Gunther men had been running the bank since founding it more than a century ago. How many times had his father drilled into him the fact that as the oldest, it was Trey's birthright, his privilege, to take over the family business?

He didn't think it was much of a privilege to come home, the ink of his college diploma barely dried, and try to make a life in a place where nearly everyone his age had fled. The dying town had felt like a trap closing in around him.

It hadn't helped to know the town was looking to Trey, as the next generation of Gunther, to save it. In fact, it scared him half to death. Trey scrubbed a hand over his face. It still did. These people were depending on him. What if he couldn't turn things around? So far, his best efforts hadn't netted any real results.

What if he failed the town and his family name?

More than once he found himself echoing the thoughts of George Bailey, the beleaguered character from that old Christmas movie. He'd felt isolated and resentful to be tied down in a backwater burg.

It wasn't fair he should have to remain behind to clean up a mess he hadn't made when everyone else had an opportunity to chase their dreams.

But life wasn't fair. And he had an obligation to his family and to the bank and to the town. *Noblesse oblige.*

So he stayed.

Trey stood and crossed to the window. He pushed aside the heavy curtain to look out on the street. Over time, Village Green had charmed him. He discovered living life at a crawl came with certain advantages. Without traffic jams and overcrowded calendars, people took time for one another.

Trey still chafed against the little inconveniences of rural life. Like having to drive thirty miles to see a movie or a dentist or eat at a restaurant where the entire menu wasn't chicken-fried. And while he'd learned to accept it, the small-town lack of privacy occasionally got on his nerves.

Bottom line, Village Green was his home. Gunther roots went deep, and he was committed. He had a good job. A good church. Good friends.

He was content.

Or at least he'd told himself he was content. Recently he'd noticed contentment had begun to feel an awful lot like boredom. His days, uninterrupted by even the slightest alteration in pattern, ran together in an uninspired blur. At twenty-eight, his life had become routine. Even dull.

Trey thought about the fury on Hallie's face when he told her she had to check in with him once a week. He smiled.

Maybe things were looking up.

CHAPTER THREE

Hallie's hands shook so hard she could barely maneuver the metal cart down the cramped aisles of the Grocery Giant. How dare her sister sign over financial responsibility to *him*? Even worse, how dare he flash her one of those smug smiles of his and then proceed to tell her that he expected her to report to him once a week?

She seethed down the canned goods aisle. She was so caught up in her mad, she bypassed the green beans and had to backtrack, which added to her snit. She snatched two cans off the shelf and slammed them into her cart.

"Not the brand you like?" Mrs. Justice, Hallie's fourth-grade teacher, happened to turn into the aisle just as Hallie's beans clanked in.

"Oh, hi, Mrs. Justice." Hallie's face heated, and she felt her neck retracting into her shoulders like a self-conscious turtle, exactly as it had done when she was ten and in Mrs. Justice's class. "No, the beans are fine. I . . . uh . . ."

Mrs. Justice gave Hallie a comforting pat. "I understand, dear. With your mother's stroke and all, I'm sure you are under a great deal of stress."

Hallie thought about her multiple run-ins with Trey and bobbed her head. "Yes, ma'am. It's been very stressful."

"How is your mother? I heard she was coming home today."

"She's better, thank you. She says she improved the minute she walked into the house."

Mrs. Justice nodded. "I know just how she feels. Nothing like being home to put everything to rights. I'd like to bring supper to you all tomorrow. Is your sister home yet?"

Hallie's hands tightened on the cart handle, bracing herself for the coming reassurance that her sister would solve everything. "Not yet."

"Well, I'll bring plenty in case she gets home by then. I imagine she'll have her husband with her. Fried chicken, okay?"

Hallie relaxed her grip and smiled. "That sounds wonderful. Thank you. We'll look forward to it."

They said their goodbyes, and Mrs. Justice wheeled away. The distraction had given Hallie's temper time to cool. What was she making such a big fuss about? She could handle the meetings with Trey. She even managed a small smile of satisfaction, knowing he would suffer through each meeting every bit as much as she would.

Hallie glanced at her watch and realized she'd been gone from home longer than she'd intended. Fearful her mother might fall, Hallie had made her promise not to get up unless it was an absolute emergency. She set off down the aisle for some serious shopping. She buzzed along, picking up speed, tossing items in her buggy and checking them off her list.

When she rounded the corner on the next to last aisle, she considered the rapidly filling cart. This seemed like an awful lot of food for just her and her mother, especially when the whole town would be delivering meals to their door.

It wasn't until she got to the "three T-bone steaks" written on the bottom of the page that she realized her mother wasn't planning on feeding just the two of them. Hallie sighed. Her mom had deluded herself into believing Janice would hurry home to take charge.

Fat chance.

Like everyone else with any sense, Janice had escaped Village Green as soon as she could. Having run through all the eligible men in town, and some of the ineligible ones, Hallie thought with a grimace, Janice had taken her charms off to Tech.

A blonde and beautiful cheerleader, Janice took five and a half years to earn her four-year degree, probably because four years wasn't nearly long enough to date all the men who were asking. After graduation, she caught the eye of Bubba Carson, a handsome ex–football star with a bum knee, who served as an assistant football coach at the school. Following a fairytale courtship, Janice and Bubba married and settled at a west Texas college where Bubba had been named head coach.

Being the wife of a coach suited Janice to a T. Since football was king in Texas, being married to a coach elevated her to small-town royalty. In season, Janice's life was a whirl of games, parties, and travel. The family only saw Janice when a television camera happened to catch her in the stadium. Off season, Janice was busy with recruitment dinners and more travel.

No way she'd carve time out of her schedule to spend it in a ghost town nursing her mother back to health.

Hallie pulled up in front of the refrigerated meat compartment and selected three thick steaks as per the instructions. She supposed she could freeze the third one for another time. She hated for her mother to be disappointed, but she knew her sister would be in no rush to come back.

When she'd marked the last item off the list, Hallie pushed her buggy to the one open cash register.

"Hey, girl!" Marilyn Bray, in her red-and-white-striped Grocery Giant shirt, greeted her from behind the register. "It's been a while. You here to take care of your mom?"

"Yeah, she's just out of rehab."

Marilyn pulled groceries out of the cart and swiped them across the scanner. She paused, green beans in hand, to give Hallie an assessing look. "You look good. Trey know you're home?"

She hesitated. *Play it cool, girl.* Marilyn was the mouthpiece for Village Green gossip. If Hallie didn't want to be the subject of erroneous rumors all over town, she needed to nip them in the bud right now.

Hallie shrugged. "Oh, sure. I was just at the bank talking with him."

"Really?" Marilyn's glittery blue eyeshadow shot up to her hairline. Apparently sensing a scoop, she set the beans on the counter to give Hallie her full attention.

"He's mom's banker," Hallie said dampeningly.

Marilyn's face fell. "Oh." She picked up the can and swept it over the scanner. Her expression suddenly turned sly. "Any chance you two will try to patch things up?"

"No way." Hallie laughed off the ridiculous thought. "Not interested."

Marilyn scanned the last few items on the conveyor belt. "I talked to your sister a while back. She told me about your great job."

Hallie could swear she felt the earth move. She had called Janice to tell her when she opened her public relations company, but she hadn't thought her sister had been impressed. Honestly, at the time she wasn't sure Janice even listened. And yet, Janice had been bragging about her? Could it be? A flicker of pleasure warmed her heart.

"I was totally impressed," Marilyn said. "She told me you do makeovers at some big department store in Fort Worth. I guess that means you get free makeup, huh?"

Hallie's brows pulled together. "Makeovers? No, I don't work at a department store. I have my own business. I run a public relations company."

"You're kidding." Marilyn packed a world of disappointment in her tone. "That's too bad. I guess that means you have to pay full price for makeup like the rest of us." She frowned and loaded the bags into Hallie's buggy. "Funny Janice would get that wrong. Seems like a sister should know stuff like that."

Not funny. The warmth in Hallie's chest cooled to a chilly ache. After all this time, it shouldn't hurt, but it did.

"So, how long are you staying?" Marilyn placed the last bag in the cart.

"Just until I can arrange care for Mom. Then I'm gone."

Hallie ran up the steps and into the house, grocery bags dangling from each hand. Her mother sat in her chair by the window just as she'd been when Hallie left over an hour and a half ago. "Oh, Mom. I'm so sorry. I hadn't planned to be gone so long. Have you been sitting there the whole time?"

She nodded. "But I haven't been lonely. People have been in and out since you left."

"I'm glad." Hallie hurried with her bags down the hall to the kitchen. She saw two freshly baked pies and a foil-wrapped mound that could be cookies sitting on the kitchen table. "Who's the food from?"

"Apple pie from the Ryders, chocolate pecan pie from Etta Greely, and chocolate chip cookies from the Dansons. I think the cookies are still warm. I thought I'd wait till you got home, and we could have some."

Hallie deposited the groceries on the table and pulled up the corner of the foil to peek inside. "They look amazing. You want me to bring you a couple?"

"Yes, please."

She put away the groceries that needed to be refrigerated, then placed two cookies on a plate for her mother and grabbed another for herself.

"Delicious." Hallie popped the last bite of her cookie into her mouth and handed the plate to her mother. "Nice and gooey."

Her mom accepted it with her good hand and propped it on her lap.

"Do you want something to drink with it?" Hallie said. "A glass of milk might be nice?"

"No, I'm fine." She bit into the soft cookie and sent pieces raining into her lap. She looked down at the mess and burst into tears.

Hallie had read enough literature about stroke victims to know that tears lay close to the surface. It didn't make it any less awful to see her mother cry.

She crouched down to her mother's level. "What is it? What's the matter?"

"Look at me," she sobbed. "I'm helpless. Worse than a baby. I can't walk. I can't use my arm. I can't even eat." She cried harder.

Hallie was familiar with the expression "parenting your parent," but until the stroke she hadn't truly understood it. Her mother's incapacity had reversed their roles. Now Hallie was the strong one. It would be her job to give comfort, soothe hurts.

She leaned in, gathered her into her arms as she would a child, and rocked her gently. "It's okay, Mom. It's okay."

"What am I going to do?" Her mother sniffled against her shoulder. "How will I manage?"

"We're going to take it one day at a time," Hallie said. "Remember what the doctor said? With therapy and exercise you will regain some use of your left arm. He thinks your coordination will improve. And as you get stronger, walking will become easier."

She met her mom's hopeful gaze and repeated the doctor's words with a confidence she didn't feel. "This is as bad as it gets."

Her mother grabbed them like a lifeline. "He said that, didn't he? That I'll improve. That this is as bad as it gets."

"Yes, ma'am." She patted her mother's knee and stood. "Why don't I clean up the crumbs and get you another cookie before I bring in the rest of the groceries."

Her mother smiled. "That's a good idea. We need to get busy if we're going to be ready when Trey gets here at six."

Hallie stiffened. "Did you just say Trey is coming *here*?"

Her mother bobbed her head.

Hallie kept her expression and voice carefully disinterested. "Why is Trey coming here?"

"I asked him to have dinner with us. It's the least I could do for him after he was so nice to drive all the way to Corsicana to bring me home from the rehab center." Her mother's smile widened. "I promised him we'd have steaks."

The three T-bones suddenly made sense.

The doctor was wrong. Things just got worse.

CHAPTER FOUR

Hallie was determined not to spend one second fixing up for Trey. After all, this wasn't a date. It was an extended nightmare.

Even so, it took her thirty minutes to settle on the perfect T-shirt and pair of shorts to wear to dinner. If she just happened to pick the ones she knew were the most flattering, so be it. Let him see what he cast aside.

While she was at it, she took time to redo her hair and makeup. Not for his benefit. As a PR specialist, she knew there was power in looking her best.

She was setting the table when she heard his knock at the front door. Her traitorous pulse jumped, and she dropped a handful of silverware onto the table in a series of ear-splitting clangs.

"Pull yourself together," Hallie muttered while she gathered the fallen flatware. Just because he couldn't seem to stay out of her life was no reason for her to become all twitchy.

She headed off to answer the door and gave herself the pep talk she gave to jangled clients. "Take a deep breath." She inhaled slowly through her nose, then exhaled through her mouth. "Remember who you are. You are confident. You are poised. You are in control and ready to handle anything that comes your way. You can do this."

Her face arranged in a cool welcome, Hallie took one last calming breath and opened the door. Her next breath caught in a gasp.

Confronted with six feet, two inches of smiling, chiseled perfection, her newly mustered confident poise took a major hit.

From the other side of the screen door, Trey paused and propped an arm on the doorframe. The smile slid off his face in degrees as his eyes made an appreciative trip from her head to her feet. The gleam of pure masculine approval in his eyes seemed to transport her through time.

Hallie felt a flash of heat, and her heart thumped wildly. She was eighteen again, looking up at the man who was the center of her universe.

Trey scrubbed a hand over his face and cleared his throat before pulling open the door. He took his first step inside and stopped short. "Nice touch."

"Hmm?" Hallie's mind hadn't yet engaged.

"Greeting me at the door with weapons. Kinda keeps things in perspective."

The bite of sarcasm in his voice jerked Hallie from her flashback stupor enough to see he stared at the steak knives and forks she clutched in her hand. She gave a short, tense laugh. "I do look like I'm armed for battle, don't I?"

"Actually, yeah." He massaged the back of his neck for a second, sighed, and regarded her steadily. "Look, I know you don't want me here anymore than I want to be here, but your mother invited me, and it was important to her that I come. So just for tonight, for the sake of your mom, let's call a truce."

If she couldn't like his tactlessness in making her sound like an unpleasant burden to be endured, she had to admire his honesty. She nodded. "You're right. She's really excited you're eating dinner with us. Okay, truce." Hallie stepped back. "Mom's sitting in the backyard. You can keep her company while I finish making dinner."

Hallie led the way, intensely aware of Trey's proximity behind her while they walked down the hall through the kitchen to the door opening to the outside.

Trey paused with his hand on the doorknob. He tipped up his chin toward the platter of steaks sitting on the counter. "I'd be happy to handle the grill work if you want."

Though she was tempted to deny him on principle because truce or no truce, he was still the enemy, the truth was she wasn't very skilled at grilling steaks. The capper on an all-time rotten day would be placing a smoking platter of three hideously charred T-bones in front of Trey and her mom. "Okay. Thanks. That would be great."

He swung open the door and stepped outside. "Let me know when you want me to put them on." He pulled it closed and trotted down the stairs and across the small patio to her mother seated on a lawn chair under a tree.

Hallie watched through the window as he crouched in front of her mom and took her hands into his while he spoke. The look of pure delight on her mother's face reinforced his earlier remark. Hallie sighed. It did mean a lot to her mother to have Trey there. To see her so happy after all the upheaval of the last month was probably worth the aggravation of spending time with him.

She hated to admit it, but maybe he was right about calling a truce. It wasn't like anything changed between the two of them, only that the hostilities would cease for a couple of hours. She could do that for her mom.

Hallie walked to the table to set out the silverware she'd been carrying. Her mother had been horrified at Hallie's earlier suggestion that paper plates and napkins were good enough for Trey and insisted instead on using the pale green placemats and cloth napkins she saved for company. A mason jar of white hydrangeas that arrived earlier from a neighbor sat in the center of the table. The overall effect was pretty and festive.

While no truce could render entertaining Trey even remotely pleasurable, having her mother home from rehab was certainly worth celebrating.

She glanced at the clock. The baked potatoes needed another twenty minutes in the oven. Since Trey was keeping her mother company, she was free to get started on the salad.

Hallie pulled lettuce and other veggies from the refrigerator and lined them up by the sink. It took her a minute to locate a bowl to use and another to find the cutting board, reminding her it had been a long time since she'd done any real cooking at her mother's house. She swallowed a guilty pang. A *really,* long time.

The back door swung open, and Hallie jumped.

Trey stepped inside. "Hey, your mom wanted some tea. Okay with you if I fix us both a drink?"

"I should have offered you something." Her heart thumped so loudly she wondered if he could hear it. "The pitcher is over there. Let me get you some glasses and ice." Hallie pulled two tall glasses from the cabinet and filled them with ice. "There's sugar on the table if you want it."

"Thanks."

Hallie opened the door for him after he poured the tea. "If the charcoal looks ready, you can start the steaks any time."

A glass in each hand, Trey headed down the stairs. "Perfect. I'll be back for them in five."

Hallie pushed the door closed and slumped against it. Her nerves were a wreck. Her heart was still racing, and the muscles in her shoulders were so tight she felt she might shatter.

She slowly straightened and rolled her shoulders backward a couple of rotations. She'd been on edge since she'd passed the sign for Village Green that morning. Throw into the mix two visits *from* Trey, one visit *to* Trey, repeated reminders that her sister alone held the keys to unlocking the universe, and a mother who needed mothering—no wonder she felt so wound up. She was probably on the verge of a well-deserved nervous breakdown.

She walked to the sink and picked up the lettuce. No way she was going to break down in front of Trey. He would surely take credit for her discomfort, and she'd promised herself a long time ago she would never give him that kind of power over her again.

Determination gave her strength. She washed the lettuce, two stalks of celery, and a handful of cherry tomatoes, stopping between each to roll her shoulders again. By the time he returned to the kitchen, she was calm enough to smile as she handed him the platter of meat. She chopped the vegetables into the bowl and carried it to the table. Another shoulder roll. She could handle this.

She added a quick prayer for backup. *Please, God, help me handle this.*

"Isn't this wonderful?" Her mother beamed at Hallie and Trey after they were all seated around the table. "I feel like it's been an age since I've been home. And two ages since Hallie's been here for supper."

"I know, and I'm sorry." Hallie could barely speak past the sudden lump of guilt wedged in her throat. "I haven't felt I could get away from work."

Trey passed her the salad. "What exactly are you doing now?"

Her mother had somehow coerced her left arm, the one most affected by the stroke, up onto the table and had managed to skewer the steak with a fork. When she picked up a knife in her right hand and tried to slice off a bite of steak, her weakened left hand lost its grip on the fork. The knife dragged the steak off the plate and onto her lap. Without the fork to stabilize it, her arm slipped off the table and swept the salad plate to the floor with a crash.

Tears sprang to her eyes.

"It's okay, Mom. No harm done." Hallie jumped up from her chair, scooped the steak from her mother's lap back onto the plate, and bent to pick up the unbroken salad plate. "Let me get you a fresh one, and we'll start over."

"And why don't you let me give you a hand with your meat." Trey scooted her meal toward his. "Seems like a woman just out of rehab shouldn't have to wrestle a steer her first day back."

"I'm sorry." Tears rolled down her cheeks. "I'm just so clumsy."

Hallie turned from the cabinet, reassurance on her lips when she saw Trey gently place his big hand on her mother's shoulder. "Ma'am, you are recovering from a stroke. I believe that entitles you to a little clumsiness."

"Here's a plate for your salad." Hallie placed it in front of her. "Let me serve you. You're probably starving."

Trey slid her mother's dinner back to her, the meat now cut into small uniform pieces, then picked up the conversation as though there had been no interruption. "So Hallie, you were telling us about your work."

Hallie flashed him a heartfelt smile of pure gratitude. He might be an interfering, egotistical Gunther, but at that moment, she could have kissed him. Bless him for making so little of her mother's mistake. "I worked in advertising after I graduated from college, but I left to concentrate on public relations. I started my own agency three years ago."

Fork poised at his mouth, Trey nodded. "That's great. What exactly does your agency do?"

Whether he asked from genuine interest or to further bury her mother's discomfort, Hallie didn't care. She was delighted to talk about her work. She wanted him to know she had landed on her feet.

Ten years ago, she'd escaped Village Green to prove something. And she had. Out from under her sister's shadow, Hallie had thrived. She'd built a life and a business she could be proud of. And she'd used the hurt and anger of his rejection to get her there.

"I do a lot of things. My clients are people who need to create or upgrade their images. I work mainly with small businesses, with the occasional artist thrown in. I'm currently coordinating an exhibition for Dan Willis, the photographer."

Trey nodded. "I've seen his work. He's amazing."

Hallie couldn't help being impressed. She didn't think much culture trickled down to the boondocks. "Dan's a great guy. And he's been terrific about me overseeing his Fort Worth premiere from Village Green." Not that she intended to be here for long.

On a day of surprises, dinner turned out to be a pleasant one. Once Hallie got past her spurt of nerves and her mother's meal had been cut into manageable bites, the evening went smoothly. Most importantly, her mom seemed genuinely pleased.

The food was delicious. The steaks were done to perfection, the potatoes buttery, and the salad crisp and refreshing. They topped off the meal with decadent chocolate pecan pie, courtesy of Etta Greenly.

Somewhere over the course of the evening, the painful tension in Hallie's shoulders eased. Which seemed strange considering she was seated at a table, sharing food and conversation with her ex. Not that she ever wanted to repeat the experience. This was a temporary truce for her mother's sake. Hallie and her nerves preferred Trey when he was miles away.

After dinner, he helped clear the dishes, then sat in the living room with her mother while Hallie loaded plates into the dishwasher. She felt very much in his debt by the time she walked him to the door a little before nine. His help and genuine kindness to her mother kindled a warm glow in her chest. With her hand on the doorknob, she paused to speak words she never expected to hear coming from her lips. "Thank you for everything."

He grinned. "That was my line. Thank you. Dinner was great."

She lowered her voice, though it was unlikely her mother could hear their conversation over the blaring television. Trey leaned toward her, his face inches from hers, so he could hear her softly spoken words. He was so close, his scent so familiar, her heart did a little jumpy thing, and she had to look away to remember what it was she wanted to say. "You were great with Mom. Really. I know things were awkward and, well, I can't tell you how much I appreciated—"

Trey placed a gentle finger under Hallie's chin and lifted it so she would meet his eyes. "It's okay. I enjoyed it."

Frozen by the butterfly-soft pressure of his fingertip, Hallie was caught in his honeyed gaze. When his focus slipped to her mouth and he shifted forward, closing the scant distance between them, memories muddled, and time slipped away. Hallie's lips parted slightly, and her eyes drifted shut.

A breathless heartbeat passed. Then another.

Nothing.

When Trey's hand dropped suddenly from beneath her chin, Hallie's eyes flew open. His eyes were wide as he took a quick step backward and cleared his throat. "You know what? I need to go. Thanks for dinner. Goodnight." He was out the door and down the stairs like a shot.

Hallie stood rooted to the spot, staring out into the night while her senses screamed Mayday! Mayday!

It was several seconds before she could pull herself together enough to close the door. And another minute before she could think clearly. What in the world was that? Have I lost my mind entirely? Was I actually considering kissing the enemy?

She slumped against the wood panel and blew out a long, noisy breath. Truce over. Until she could get out of Village Green, it was war.

CHAPTER FIVE

Monday morning at his desk in the bank, Trey scrolled down the list of overdue loans, relieved to see it was short this month. The economy was tough all over, but in Village Green it was downright pitiful. Jobs were scarce and opportunities few. Unless things changed, he knew the situation would only get worse.

As a community leader, and a Gunther, he felt responsible. This was his town. These were his people. The names on the list weren't just customers, they were friends and neighbors. It wasn't that he harbored any weird delusions, like believing his family alone could save the town from imminent destruction, but he did think that as a Gunther there ought to be something he could do, some idea he could contribute to spark economic change.

Over the years he'd tried different tactics to turn things around. He'd scoured business journals, consulted with neighboring community leaders, and logged countless hours on the internet looking for ideas. He'd spearheaded committees, organized promotions, and spent the first Thursday of every month in chamber of commerce meetings trying to come up with a plan to breathe life into the dying town.

He'd prayed, begging God to show him a way to turn things around, until his knees ached.

The net impact of his efforts on the economy of Village Green was always the same. Zip. Zero. Zilch.

Frustration over his repeated failures was taking its toll. Lately he wondered if maybe the situation was hopeless.

Honestly, what could one man do?

Sighing, he turned back to his list. Bank policy was to email each person on the overdue loan list a short form letter to serve as a gentle reminder they'd missed a payment. The email was usually enough of a nudge to get a check in the mail. On the rare occasion when a loan went sixty days past due, Trey handled the matter personally.

Today, only one loan was sixty days in arrears—the mortgage on Elmer and Helen West's farm.

Trey frowned. Elmer had died two months ago after a painful, three-year battle with colon cancer. Helen had quit her job to stay home and care for him. According to Trey's records, the Wests had no insurance to cover the mortgage in the event anything happened to either of them.

Trey had been by Helen's place a couple of times since the funeral to deliver food from his mother and to see if Helen needed anything. Each time, she'd politely thanked him for the food and the offer and assured him he didn't need to worry, that she was getting by just fine. Because he understood pride, he'd stepped back to let her work through the grief and handle things on her own. Because he understood how quickly troubles compounded, he knew it was time to step in.

He pushed the intercom button. "Miss Tillie?"

"I copy, Mr. Gunther."

Trey grinned. Ever since Miss Tillie had taken up reading military thrillers, she'd adopted a sort of fractured service lingo when they spoke over the intercom. "How does my schedule look for tomorrow?"

"Copy that. Let me look. You've got a breakfast meeting with Sam at 0700 hours and a meeting with the board at 1600 hours."

"No client appointments?"

"Negative, Mr. Gunther. Were you expecting any?"

Hallie Nichols came to mind. "No, not really. Would you make me an appointment with Helen West for some time this week? Tell her I'll come out to her place if that's better for her."

"Roger. Appointment with Helen West. Anything else?"

"That's it. Thanks."

"Ten-four. Over and out."

So Hallie hadn't called for her first week's check-in. No surprises there. Trey figured he'd have to drag her kicking and screaming into his office if he wanted to meet with her. He sat back, allowing himself a moment to contemplate a wrestling match with Hallie. He ran a finger around his suddenly restrictive collar. Maybe it was better if she didn't come in.

Like it or not, she was still one very powerful temptation.

Case in point, Saturday night. He'd gone to dinner at the Nichol's out of a sense of obligation to her mother. Period. Hallie played no part in his decision to accept the invitation.

Her digs about his family were still fresh in his mind when he'd arrived at their home that evening. He'd chuckled to himself when he trotted up the front porch steps, remembering how sweet it had been to play the big, bad Gunther earlier at the bank and shake up Hallie's annoyingly cool composure. Then she'd opened the door and . . . he'd forgotten his own name.

It was only a T-shirt and pair of shorts, for heaven's sake, but he'd been thankful for a doorjamb to lean on to keep from falling over. Hallie left Village Green as a girl, but she'd come home 100 percent woman. He could almost laugh about it now, but it wasn't too funny at the time to have beads of sweat popping out on his forehead at the sight of her. Pathetic.

His first reaction, when oxygen began slowly filtering back to his brain, was annoyance. She meant nothing to him. So why, when he saw her, did he feel like a starving man looking at a feast?

The evening had gone downhill from there. He'd have been okay if he'd stayed annoyed, but it had been tough to hang on to his attitude when he'd watched Hallie with her mother. Whatever his personal feelings for Hallie, there was no denying she'd walked into a tough situation and was handling it with gentleness and courage.

By dessert, he'd made a reluctant slide from irritation to admiration.

Still, admiration didn't mean he had any business kissing her. This was the woman who had messed him over royally. Not only had she rejected him and everything he stood for, she thought he was a monster. Where was his famed Gunther pride?

Rejection and monsters, and even dignity, evaporated the instant she looked up at him with those big brown eyes when they said their whispered goodbyes at the door. Rational thought slipped away as the sweet, subtle fragrance that was uniquely Hallie reached his nostrils. In that instant, she wasn't the cool and aloof Hallie he'd written off years ago. She was the warm and vulnerable Hallie whom he'd once loved. Things were a bit fuzzy from there. The best he could figure, some sort of fog must have settled over him and addled his brain.

So, like a moron, he'd almost kissed her.

Almost.

It had been a near thing. He couldn't pinpoint what snapped him out of his stupor and diverted him from his near-disastrous trajectory, but when he came to his senses, millimeters from Hallie's tempting mouth, he'd reared back and fled from the house like a man pursued by demon hordes.

He'd probably looked as stupid as he felt, but it didn't matter. Bottom line, the crisis was averted, albeit narrowly. More importantly, he was a wiser man.

He'd fallen for her once. He would never make that mistake again.

Trey propped his elbows on the desk and scrubbed his hands over his face. He'd told himself he was punishing Hallie by forcing her to meet with him. Now he wasn't so sure who was punishing whom.

His phone rang. "Mr. Gunther, Hallie Nichols is here," Miss Tillie said. "She wants to know if you have a minute to speak with her about her mother's accounts."

Speak of the devil. "Send her in."

Trey stood behind his desk. He rolled his shoulders to work out the sudden kinks and adopted an expression of professional nonchalance as the door swung open. "Hallie, what can I do for you?"

She walked in, stopping between the leather chairs in front of his desk, and braced a hand on the seat back. This morning she'd dressed simply in a white shirt and snug-fitting blue jeans so dark they almost looked black. Instead of cowboy boots like the locals, she wore high heels. She looked classy and big city. And clearly ill at ease, whether because of Saturday's near-kiss or the fact she didn't have an appointment, he couldn't tell.

"I got some names of assisted living centers and home health care agencies from Mom's doctor this morning." Hallie looked everywhere but at him. "I didn't want to make any calls until I knew where she stands financially."

Trey nodded. "Makes sense."

Her gaze came to rest on the stack of papers on his desk, and she frowned. "You're busy. If this is a bad time, I can make an appointment and come back."

Trey glanced at his watch. Eleven thirty. He had half a dozen reports to do and a customer coming in at one. He'd be justified in sending her away, might even get some pleasure from it, but then she'd just have to come back. Something told him it would be better to get the meeting over with.

It probably wouldn't hurt to hold their meeting in a public place. He wasn't as likely to be flummoxed by a pair of big brown eyes in a room full of eager witnesses.

"I've got a full schedule, but I'll tell you what I can do. I was about to grab something to eat. I can print out your mother's account information, and we can look at it over lunch."

She pushed a strand of dark hair behind her ear, exposing a delicate gold earring. "I don't know . . ."

Trey bent in front of his computer to call up Mrs. Nichols's account and send it to the printer. "It's up to you." He straightened and gave her an indifferent shrug as the machine purred to life. "If lunch isn't good for you, then we can schedule something later in the week."

He watched the emotions warring on Hallie's face. It was obvious she didn't want to eat lunch with him, but she was eager to find living arrangements for her mother. If she delayed their meeting, she'd have to stay in town longer. And she'd made it abundantly clear how she felt about that.

Talk about a rock and a hard place.

He pulled the paperwork from the printer and tapped it against his hand. "What's it going to be?"

"Lunch is fine."

The tension he heard in her voice said it was anything but. He nodded. "Let me tell Miss Tillie my plans, and we can be on our way."

Hallie and Trey didn't speak when he led them from his office like an executioner with his prisoner, side by side through the bank lobby and out into the March sunlight. As they stepped onto the pavement, Trey slipped on his sunglasses and lifted his face to let the warmth wash over him.

He loved this time of year. To his way of thinking, March in Texas was about as close to heaven as a man could get without dying. The warmer weather meant the start of a new softball season. By the middle of the month, spring had arrived in a rush of color and scent. Everything felt fresh and clean and new. Anything was possible.

"Where are we going?"

He almost laughed. It was obvious Hallie had been away a long time if she thought they had a choice of restaurants. "Estelle's Diner. We can walk by the Green."

The Green, for which Village Green was named, was a large square of land, two city blocks by two city blocks, in the center of town. The land had been designated as a city park by the founding fathers a hundred years ago. To Trey, it was a symbol of everything that was good about the community.

Bound on all four sides by ancient wrought iron fences and concrete sidewalks, the Green was a grassy oasis. Clusters of oak trees, planted long ago, now towered over the land and the thick canopies of leafy green provided welcome shade when the inevitable heat of summer rolled around.

Today, and every day the weather cooperated, people were enjoying the park. Several strolled in pairs, and a couple of the old benches were occupied.

Sunday, after church, things really came alive as residents sat under the trees to watch the weekly softball game. Just looking across the Green filled Trey with a deep sense of pleasure and pride.

"Doesn't change much, does it?"

The tone of Hallie's voice reminded him that not everyone appreciated his idyllic community. Hallie despised his "one-horse town." But that hadn't always been true. She'd once loved Village Green. Just as she'd once loved him.

While they traveled along the sidewalk in strained silence, it was hard to believe there had ever been anything but animosity between them, but Trey remembered it clearly. Hallie had once loved him. No. She hadn't just loved him. She'd adored him.

Back then, she'd hung on his every word, as though what he'd said really mattered. The memory made him smile. She'd listened to his plans, believed in his dreams.

Talk about power. Hallie's love had made him invincible.

At eighteen, she had been his world. Thoughts of her filled his mind from the time he woke in the morning until he fell asleep at night. Hallie had been the joy of his present, the hope of his future. He'd loved her with every ounce of his being. And even as an eighteen-year-old, he'd somehow understood the love they shared was an amazing gift.

What he hadn't understood was it wasn't his to keep.

In an instant he was transported back to the summer of his eighteenth year. College loomed large on the horizon, but for a few lazy months, time had stood still.

Trey remembered there'd been a heat wave that had all the old folks griping about the weather. Since the high temperatures meant Hallie wore little T-shirts and next-to-nothing shorts, he'd seen no reason to complain.

Hallie's sister, Janice, was home from college, stirring up trouble, as usual. Trey never believed Janice was mean, just bored, and determined to draw attention to herself. She was the kind of person who needed attention like an addict needed drugs. She'd hit on Trey a couple of times, nothing serious. Janice hit on everyone. Trey had been so full of Hallie, he'd hardly noticed.

His thoughts suddenly shifted to the August night when the bottom dropped out.

He'd played a softball game earlier that evening, pitched a winning game against the previously unbeaten team from Corsicana. By the time he'd driven home, showered, and dressed, he was late for his date with Hallie. He'd lent his truck to his younger brother, so Trey had decided to cut across the Green to save time getting to her house.

His mind wandered while he hurried, split between replaying highlights from the night's game, and anticipating the cuddling he was about to do with his girl. He'd been startled to hear someone call his name from the old gazebo. The voice had sounded enough like Hallie's that he'd trotted up the rickety wooden stairs to investigate.

Trey never did figure out what Janice had been doing alone on the gazebo that night, but by the time he'd deflected her latest advances and convinced her that he had plans with her sister, he was another fifteen minutes late.

He could see Hallie was steamed when she'd answered the door. None of the usual delight at seeing him sprang to her eyes. She'd been breathing hard, as if she'd run a long way, and her normally sunny expression had been shuttered and cool. For a second, he'd thought she'd been crying.

She'd agreed to sit on the porch swing with him, but he remembered she'd moved so far to the opposite edge, he'd feared she'd fall off.

That's when she dropped the bomb.

"We need to talk."

He'd scooted closer and grinned. "I was hoping we could do more than talk."

The fact that she hadn't smiled as she shoved away the arm he'd slid behind her should have warned him there was trouble ahead.

"I'm serious, Trey." Her voice strangely flat, she said, "I saw . . ." She paused and cleared her throat. "I've made a decision, and I think you should know."

Seeing there would be no snuggling until she got whatever was bothering her off her chest, he'd agreed. "Go ahead. I'm listening."

"I'm not going to college with you."

"Look, if this is because I was late, I'm sorry. I know I should have called—"

Hallie had shaken her head but continued staring at her hands clasped in her lap, obviously to avoid meeting his eyes. "It's not about being late. It's about wanting different things."

"That's just crazy. I want you."

She'd continued in that same toneless voice, as if she hadn't heard him. "I need to get away from here."

When it finally penetrated his mind that she was serious, a cold panic seized him. He'd gripped her hands. "No. No, you don't. I love you. You know that. You belong here with me in Village Green."

For the first time all evening, she'd made eye contact. Even in the shadows he had seen that her normally sparkling eyes were dull. Expressionless. "Not anymore. There is nothing here for me." Her eyes had filled with tears, and she stood to go into the house.

Truly scared, he'd reached for her hands. "No, Hallie. Don't leave. We need to talk."

"There's nothing left to say. I'm leaving."

"But why?" He held tight when she tried to pull away.

"Don't you get it?" Tears streamed down her face, and her breath caught in ragged sobs.

"I hate—I hate this one-horse town!"

CHAPTER SIX

Trey's memories of the rest of that night, the rest of that summer, were vague. He remembered thinking none of it was real, that at any moment he'd awaken from the nightmare.

He knew Hallie loved him and Village Green too much to turn her back on them. She'd never go through with it. No way.

And, when she left without a word or a backward glance, he remembered the pain.

A gust of warm air brushed across his face, easing the tension in his jaw, and returning him to the present. It had been a long time since he'd allowed himself to relive that particular part of his past.

Trey absently massaged a hand over his heart. No wonder he avoided those memories. Hallie had cut him so deeply, lacerated his pride so completely, the memories still had the power to hurt. Even ten years later.

He and Village Green were irrevocably linked. And Hallie had cruelly rejected them both.

He'd been crushed at first. Devastated. In time, the pain gave way to anger. How could she say she loved him one minute, then turn her back on him and the plans they'd made the next? Finally, anger cooled to indifference. He'd obviously been wrong about Hallie. She hadn't truly loved him. She wasn't the woman he'd thought she was. Eventually he'd reasoned away his feelings for her until Hallie was nothing more than a girl he'd once dated, a mistake he'd once made.

So here they were, two people whose lives intersected unexpectedly after a decade of separation, tied by a painful history best forgotten. No wonder she didn't want to eat lunch with him. He'd definitely lost his appetite.

Obviously, her opinion of him hadn't improved, but he wondered if after all this time, Hallie had at least come to appreciate the unique charms of Village Green. Surely a woman who lived with the crowds and traffic of the city would acknowledge the appeal of the slower-paced community.

Trey looked around, trying to see his town from her perspective. Hallie stumbled, and he instinctively reached for her elbow to steady her. "You okay?"

"Yeah, I didn't see the pothole."

She'd caught the heel of her high-heeled shoe in a deep crack in the uneven pavement. He glanced ahead of them and frowned. How had he not noticed the sidewalk bordering the Green resembled a war zone?

When had ragged-edged weeds started springing up at regular intervals through breaks in the crumbling concrete? A little wear added to the historic flavor of the community, certainly, but holes large enough to swallow pets and small children were probably taking the whole antiquity thing to the extreme. Not to mention exposing the town to potential lawsuits.

He would bring it up at the next council meeting. When she'd freed her shoe, Trey released her arm, and they continued toward the restaurant.

While they walked, he resumed his surreptitious inspection. On a positive note, the grass on the Green was newly mown. Unfortunately, the city's tractor mower was too large and unwieldy to cut close to obstacles in its path, so thick clumps of tall grass were left to grow up beside the benches and trees. Trey grimaced. Even to the town's staunchest supporter, it wasn't a great look. The stretches of smooth lawn interrupted by longer tufts of grass gave the unflattering effect of a poodle with a bad haircut. He darted a quick glance at Hallie, knowing it was too much to hope she wouldn't notice.

Across Main Street, to their right, was the downtown area of Village Green. Trey had always regarded the faded orange-brick buildings as pieces of living history, but today, trying to view them through Hallie's undoubtedly critical eyes, he realized the buildings looked less like history and more like candidates for a wrecking ball. Though structurally sound, there was no denying the whole block looked shabby and dilapidated.

He kept a collection of framed, nostalgic, old black-and-white photos of downtown Village Green hanging on the walls in the bank lobby. In the pictures, shoppers strolled the busy sidewalks beneath wide awnings, admiring the merchandise displayed behind the spotless windows of shop after shop. Ruffled curtains and flower-filled pots lining the sills brought life to the apartments above the stores. There was even a photograph of a traffic jam.

The last traffic jam on Main Street had been cleared away long before he was born.

Today there were only a handful of businesses left. The awnings were gone, and most of the windows were boarded up with sheets of graying plywood. Paint peeled in faded strips from the sills of the abandoned second story flats.

He didn't need Hallie to tell him what he could see for himself. Village Green looked like a disaster.

He frowned. When did things get this bad? How had he missed seeing it? He walked this same path nearly every day. Had he let his pride blind him to the deteriorated reality staring him in the face?

He hated seeing the town this way. Worse, he hated that Hallie should see it. He stole a glance. Was she gloating as she walked beside him, patting herself on the back for escaping when she did? Honestly, the way things looked right now, he couldn't blame her. The situation seemed hopeless. Escape sounded pretty appealing.

They crossed the road and stepped up onto the sidewalk in front of Estelle's. Judging by the number of cars parked along the street, the restaurant had a big lunch crowd. Trey pulled open the glass door and stood aside so Hallie could enter ahead of him. While she stepped past, he breathed a prayer. *"Okay, Lord, it's worse than I thought. The town's a wreck. Your Word says the fervent prayer of a righteous man availeth much, and believe me, right now I'm all over the fervent thing. We've got to have Your help. We've got to turn things around. I'm desperate, Lord. I need a plan."*

CHAPTER SEVEN

Tinny bells jingled against the glass door signaling Hallie's entrance into Estelle's Café. The pungent odor of grease and onions and a thousand memories bombarded her when she stepped inside the old diner. She blinked twice to adjust from bright sun to fluorescent light, then paused at the near-antique cash register on the front counter, waiting for a hostess to seat them.

Trey laid his hand on her shoulder, and she could hear the amusement in his voice when he leaned down and whispered, "No big city frills here. Estelle expects us to find our own table."

"For a second I'd forgotten just how far I am from civilization." She sucked in a deep breath for courage and started across the scarred, black-and-white-checked floor, dismayed to see every table in the front of the long rectangular room was taken.

Trey raised his voice to be heard over the din of a dozen-plus conversations underscored by an upbeat country music soundtrack. "I see an open spot in the back."

Feeling the weight of the scrutiny of the diners, she regretted her decision to join him for lunch. She should never have agreed to meet him in such a public place. It was bound to stir up gossip. She should have made an appointment to see him in his office at a later date. However, she was impatient for the information he had, the facts about her mother's finances that could free her from Village Green.

Hallie moved quickly down the narrow aisle between tables toward her goal, the free booth in the back of the restaurant, when the Ryders waved them over to their table. The retired couple had been friends of her family forever. Pretending she didn't see them was not an option. Nor was it possible. Mrs. Ryder had always preferred bold colors and lots of sparkle. Today the plus-sized, older woman wore a bright floral top paired with fuchsia pants and several rhinestone barrettes clipped in her dyed black hair.

"What a nice surprise to see you two. Together." Mrs. Ryder looked pointedly from Hallie to Trey and back to Hallie, a gleam of interest in her eyes.

Hallie could almost see the matchmaking wheels spinning in Mrs. Ryder's head. "Trey is Mother's banker." She spoke loud enough for the information to carry to any interested parties seated in the room. "We're here to look over her papers."

Trey shook hands with Mr. Ryder and nodded toward Hallie in confirmation. "This is purely a business lunch."

"Well, hmmm." The speculative light in Mrs. Ryder's eyes dimmed, but apparently she wasn't ready to release her captives. "How is your mother, Hallie? You were out of church so fast yesterday, we didn't get a chance to speak with her."

Guilty as charged. As the last amen fell from the pastor's lips, Hallie had her mother by the arm, practically dragging her to the nearest exit. "I'm sorry we missed you. I know Mom wanted to thank you for the delicious apple pie you sent, but she tires so easily since her stroke, I had to take her home as soon as the service was over."

Though her mother was no doubt fatigued, the rushed escape wasn't entirely for her benefit. Honestly, Hallie just couldn't face all those people. "I'm sure she'll be calling to thank you."

The stack of glittering plastic bangles on her wrist clattered as Mrs. Ryder dismissed the suggestion with a sweep of her hand.

"Bless her heart, she doesn't need to thank me. It was my pleasure. Your mother always had a fondness for my apple pie."

Mr. Ryder leaned toward Hallie. "You know, the Mrs. and I were saying we hardly recognized you on Sunday." He chuckled. "Who'd have guessed such a pretty girl was hiding under all that hair you used to wear?"

"Mason!" Mrs. Ryder swatted her husband's hand. She looked back to Hallie and rolled her eyes. "Ignore him. I know he meant it as a compliment, no matter how badly it came out."

"I don't need an interpreter," he said. "The girl knows a compliment when she hears one. What I'm saying is you've turned into a real beauty. I believe you could give your sister some serious competition."

How many times as a teenager had she hoped to hear those words? Dreamed of being acknowledged and affirmed? Even so, the knowledge that the entire restaurant was listening had her flushing up to her hairline. "Thank you."

"How is Janice?" Mrs. Ryder asked, mercifully changing the subject. "We haven't seen her in ages. We've been expecting her to come home to take care of your poor mother."

"Hallie can take care of things here." Trey clapped a hand on Hallie's shoulder. "She's used to being in charge. I don't know if you heard, but she runs her own public relations company in Fort Worth."

"You don't say?" Mr. Ryder rocked back in his chair, slapped his hands on his thighs and crowed with delight. "Beauty and brains." By now his deep voice was so loud, Hallie was certain they could hear him bellowing halfway down the street. "Hallie, you are what they call a late bloomer."

Mrs. Ryder leaned across the table to whack him again. "Mercy, Mason, that isn't the sort of thing a young lady likes to hear."

Trey applied gentle pressure on Hallie's arm, encouraging her to move on. "It's great to talk to you, but Hallie and I have a lot to cover, so I think we'd better get down to work."

Mrs. Ryder gave them an airy wave of dismissal. "Don't let us keep you. Trey, tell your family hello for us. Hallie, be sure to give our best to your mother."

After goodbyes, Hallie and Trey made it to the back of the restaurant without further interruption. Hallie didn't think it was disinterest that cleared their path, rather everyone had been brought up-to-date by eavesdropping on her overloud conversation with the Ryders.

That's how it was in a small town. People thought they had a right to know everyone else's business.

Hallie halted at the empty booth, suddenly swamped with a hundred memories. She and Trey had logged a lot of hours at this particular Formica-topped table.

In a town the size of Village Green where date spots were severely limited, Estelle's was the premier hangout. Unlike couples who chose seats in the front of the diner so they could be seen, she and Trey had favored the relative privacy in the back. They would sit on the same side of the booth, hip pressed to hip, and hands linked beneath the cover of the table.

Funny, after all this time, she remembered so clearly how it had felt to hold his hand. The strength of his long fingers interlocked with hers was comfortable, yet strangely unsettling. The warmth of his touch was peaceful, yet unbelievably exciting.

Trey coughed. "Brings back memories, doesn't it?"

Hallie sincerely hoped her expression had not revealed the direction of her thoughts. Under no circumstances would she go there with him. Though her face heated, she shrugged as if she had no idea what he was talking about. "Not really."

Thankfully, he chose not to press his point and extended a hand in invitation. "Have a seat."

Hallie waited until he moved toward one bench before making an obvious point of selecting the seat on the opposite side.

"What? You don't want to sit here by me?" Trey's smile was mischievous as he patted the place beside him.

"Not even a little."

"You won't be able to hear me very well from over there."

She resisted the temptation to smile at his playfully wheedling tone. "I'll take my chances."

He picked up two laminated menus from behind the chrome napkin dispenser and handed one to Hallie. "I recommend the plate lunch. Monday is pot roast, mashed potatoes, and green beans."

"Monday was pot roast, mashed potatoes, and green beans ten years ago." Hallie scanned the menu front and back, then looked over the top of it at Trey in wide-eyed amazement. "Do you realize, other than the prices, not one thing on this menu has changed in a decade?"

He shot her a cocky grin. "You know what they say. When you've got a winner, you stick with it."

"I wonder if there is a saying about being so deeply stuck in a rut you can't see your way out of it." She hadn't meant her remark as an indictment of Trey's life, but she could tell by his pained look that he took it as one.

They stared at their menus in uneasy silence.

Darn it. She hadn't meant to insult him. Especially after he'd championed her in front of the nosey lunch crowd.

"Thanks for helping me out back there." She inclined her head toward the Ryders.

"No problem." His gaze remained trained on the menu.

The stony look on his face confirmed she'd wounded him with her careless remark. "When I said that about being stuck in a rut, I wasn't talking about you. I was just . . ." She sighed, then started over. "I'm sorry. I really appreciate you mentioning my company. If I'm going to be the main topic of gossip, I'd at least like people to get their facts straight."

He still didn't look up, but the comment earned her a half smile.

Estelle Rangely, the sixty-something owner of the diner, arrived at the booth with a pencil and small pad of paper. "Hey, Trey. What can I get—" Her gaze traveled to Hallie, and her brows shot high. "Hallie?"

"Yeah, hi, Estelle. It's me."

Estelle pushed her reading glasses farther down on her nose and peered over the top to get a better look. "I hardly recognized you. You look different." She studied her a moment longer. "You look good."

Since Estelle didn't have a mean bone in her body, Hallie chose to take the remark as a compliment. "Thanks. I'm surprised to see you're still here. Weren't you planning on selling out and moving to Florida?"

"You offering to buy?"

Hallie laughed. "Sorry. I'm just passing through."

Estelle heaved a theatrical sigh. "Then I guess I'm staying." She pushed her glasses back into place. "What can I get you two?"

Trey looked at Hallie and hitched up a brow. "Plate lunch?"

She nodded.

Trey flashed Estelle one of his charm-packed smiles. "Make that two plate lunches and a couple of iced teas, please."

Estelle wrote down the order and stuck the pencil behind her ear. "Coming right up."

Trey waited until she walked away before leaning into the table and saying softly, "I'm really sorry about all this. I would never have suggested Estelle's had I known you were going to be grilled and insulted by every person in the place. I guess I've grown accustomed to the entire town butting into my life, but you've been away long enough it's got to be a shock to discover a change of hairstyle makes front page news."

The apology felt nice, like cooling salve on a bee sting. "I haven't been gone that long. I remember all too well what it's like to live in a fishbowl." Because he looked genuinely embarrassed for her, she smiled to lighten the mood. "It's a pleasant change to hear compliments, though. All I used to get was unflattering comparisons to Janice."

Estelle delivered two tall, red, plastic tumblers of iced tea to the table. Hallie dumped a couple packages of yellow sweetener into her glass and stirred.

When she looked up, Trey's eyes were on her. "For what it's worth, I don't think people mean to be unkind."

It had taken a lot of years before she'd arrived at the same conclusion. She shook her head. "No, I don't think so, either. They've known me all my life. They believe having watched me grow up somehow entitles them to meddling rights." She blew out a breath before continuing. "Do you know what bothers me the most? Knowing some of what they say about me is true. I *did* hide behind my hair. I actually styled it so my bangs would cover what, like a third of my face. It was like wearing a curtain. Who does that?"

Once she started talking, she couldn't stop. The confessions rolled off her tongue in one embarrassing wave after another. "Janice was so outgoing and beautiful and popular, I couldn't compete. What was the point? So I deliberately faded into the background. I guess I figured being invisible was better than being criticized."

Hallie forced a laugh to dispel the painful memory. "It's pretty ironic the kid who specialized in invisibility is now the one teaching others to stand out."

Trey gave her a long measuring look before he spoke. "I don't know. I think someone who'd been overlooked would be especially attuned to others in the same position. Your experience qualifies you to help them avoid the same trap."

Hallie blinked. She didn't know what she'd expected from Trey, but it certainly wasn't sensitivity and insight. What did a guy loaded with looks and charm know about people who lived in the shadows? Evidently plenty. He'd immediately grasped what had taken her years to understand.

Her childhood, good or bad, had prepared her for life. She was intimately aware of the habits, mannerisms, and dress that made a person "disappear" and consequently knew what it would take to stand out. Over time she discovered those basic concepts, when tweaked, worked equally well for companies.

He regarded her over the rim of his tea glass. "Sounds like your job is a good fit."

She nodded. She loved her job. She loved her clients and knowing she made a difference in their lives and businesses. That she mattered. "It is. It's great to feel I'm providing an important service to my clients. Speaking of which, the clock is ticking. I need to figure out what to do with my mother so I can get back to my work, and you can get back to yours."

"True." Trey pulled out the papers he'd printed at the bank and laid them on the table, positioning the pages at an angle so they both could read them.

"This amount is your mother's savings." He pulled a pen from his shirt pocket and pointed to the number at the base of a long column. "In addition, she has money coming in from your father's retirement pension, social security benefits, and dividends from her investments."

He paused, discreetly sliding a sheet of paper over the printout when Estelle approached. She placed two loaded plates on the table and smiled. "Enjoy."

"Wow, this smells amazing." Hallie hadn't thought she was hungry, but the pot roast looked delicious. She didn't eat much comfort food back in Fort Worth. She tasted a bite. "It *is* amazing. Estelle has definitely not lost her touch." She forked up another piece before pushing aside the cover sheet. "What kind of investments does my mother have?"

Trey pointed to a list of corporations on the center of the page. "Your father and I worked up a wide-spectrum portfolio of stocks and bonds before he died. We invested pretty conservatively, and while it's not a lot, it brings in a steady income."

Hallie studied the list with a frown. "I don't claim to know much about investments, but I do know they don't manage themselves." She lifted her gaze to him. "Who handles Mom's portfolio?"

He lifted his chin. "Me."

Her brows shot up. "I didn't know the bank provided investment services for its customers."

"The bank doesn't. I do. And I don't do it for most of my customers. But I do it for your mom."

There was no mistaking the defensiveness in his voice. "Oh."

After a beat of unblinking silence, he said, "If it's a problem, I can always turn them over to Janice."

She rolled her eyes. "Now there's a recipe for disaster."

He picked up his fork and turned his focus to his meal as if her decision made no difference to him. "Then let me continue to handle it."

It made sense. On money matters, Trey was the expert. By the looks of the figures in front of her, he had a real knack for making a profit. He was not only knowledgeable, but he was also convenient. The bank was only blocks from her mother's house. And, in matters of business, at least, Trey was someone she could trust.

It pained her to admit it, but he was clearly the best man for the job. He was capable, convenient, and trustworthy, so why was she hesitating?

Because this was war and Trey was the enemy. After her reaction to him the other night, she'd promised herself she wouldn't give him even a toehold into her life.

He must have sensed her internal debate. "I know you want to wrap things up as quickly as possible, but there's no reason you have to make a decision today." He pointed to the documents. "You've got the information you need to make arrangements for your mother. You can get back to me about how you'd like to handle her investments."

"Thanks."

Hallie picked up the papers and read over the financial details while they finished their lunch—partly because she needed the information to move forward, but mostly to avoid making conversation with Trey. Fraternizing with the enemy seemed risky at best.

The numbers looked good. As in better than she'd dared to hope. Much better. Based on the preliminary figures she'd gathered about healthcare and living expenses, her mother had enough income each month from social security, the pension, and her investments to live comfortably without dipping into her savings. Hallie set down the report with a loud sigh.

Trey tipped up a brow. "Problem?"

"No. Relief. Pure, unadulterated relief." Joy bubbled up, expanding inside her until she was almost giddy with it. A grin stretched across her face. She was free. "I really had no idea about Mom's financial situation. I came here half afraid you'd tell me she's broke. The last couple of nights, I've actually had nightmares about giving up my apartment in Fort Worth and moving back to take care of her."

He lowered his fork. "And moving to Village Green would be the end of the world?"

"How can you even ask?" Hallie shuddered. "Yes, it would be the end of the world. The end of the universe. We're talking complete annihilation."

His mouth compressed into a hard line. "Then I'm glad I was able to set your mind at rest."

"Wow." Hallie blew out a slow, noisy breath and rolled the last remnant of tension from her shoulders. "This is so great. I feel like celebrating." She tapped the screen of her phone to check the time. "Can you stay for dessert? I'm buying."

"How can I refuse an offer like that?" He motioned to Estelle, bringing her back to the table. "We are splurging on dessert today. What have you got?"

"Chocolate cake. I made it just this morning." She grinned. "I don't think I'm overselling it to say it's three layers of fudgy perfection."

He caught Hallie's enthusiastic nod of approval. "We'll take two pieces, please."

Hallie's heart was so light, she felt she could afford to be magnanimous. "Thank you, Trey."

"No problem. I'm always up for dessert."

She chuckled and shook her head. "I'm talking about Mom's finances. I'm not sure I've thanked you properly for taking care of things." She knew for a fact that not only had she not thanked him, but she'd actually been rude to him. She looked away, unable to meet his eyes while she confessed. "I wasn't too happy to find out Janice had turned everything over to you."

"Not too happy?" Trey threw back his head and laughed. "You know, Hallie, I didn't remember you having such a gift for understatement."

Her face heated at the memory of storming into his office. "Okay, I admit it. I was furious." She glared at him. "Satisfied? The point is I realize it was the best move we could have made. You've done a good job. A great job. I . . . uh . . . I owe you."

He laughed again. "I wish you could have seen your face just now. It looked like you were about to choke. Pretty hard to get those words out, huh?"

This time she laughed with him. "You'll never know."

Estelle delivered two pieces of cake and the check. Hallie and Trey dug in, eating in comfortable silence.

Trey finished first. "While we're enjoying this rare moment of harmony, I think I'd like to collect."

Her smile faltered. She couldn't quite trust the look on his face. "Huh?"

"You said you owed me." He pushed his empty cake plate to the side. "Relax. I just want to pick your brain."

She narrowed her eyes. "About what?"

"About Village Green." He folded his hands on the table. "And don't tell me you don't have any ideas. As our most outspoken detractor, I'm guessing you have plenty of suggestions about things we can do to improve the town."

"Sure. That's easy. Bulldoze it."

He leveled a reproving look at her. "Very funny. Come on. I want to know what you think it would take to get us on the road to recovery."

She blinked. A really big miracle? "How would I know?"

His mouth flattened. "You're the hotshot image consultant, aren't you? Haven't you been telling me what a wizard you are in public relations?"

Had she used the word wizard? She didn't think so. But she had laid it on pretty thick about her skills. "I work with people or small companies, not entire towns."

He shrugged. "What's the difference? From what I've heard you say, building an image for a client is about branding. Your job is to present them in the best possible light, right?"

"That's an oversimplification, but yes."

"Why couldn't you do the same thing with a town?"

Something about the way he said it made Hallie think he doubted her abilities. She scooted forward on the bench and sat up a little straighter. "It's not that I couldn't do it. It's just I've never considered anything like it before."

"Fine. I'm asking you to consider it now. Suppose Village Green approached you about improving its image. What would you do?"

"Before or after I collected my fee?" She chuckled.

"You've decided to waive your fees. You're taking on the town as a charity case."

He almost sounded serious. She frowned, unsure how to proceed. Did Mr. Civic Pride really want her advice? That would be a first. She searched his face. From the intensity of his expression, it appeared he was genuinely interested. "Okay, well, the first thing I do with a new client is sit down and talk with them about their goals. What do they want to accomplish? What is the image they want to project? We come out of our first meeting with a list of clear-cut objectives."

"Makes sense." Trey pulled a folded piece of paper from his jacket pocket and scribbled GOALS, CLEAR-CUT OBJECTIVES at the top.

Her gaze traveled from the page to his eyes. "You're taking notes?"

"What can I say? I have a rotten memory." He waited a few beats, his focus on the paper in front of him, then lifted an expectant gaze to her. "Okay, then what?"

"After we outline our objectives, we look at physical appearances. Does the client's appearance confirm or negate the image we want to promote? It can be something minor, like a hairstyle change, or the decision whether or not to wear glasses. Sometimes, we do a complete wardrobe overhaul. We also look at spoken and body language."

Trey wrote APPEARANCE.

"After we are satisfied the client's appearance is in line with the image we want to convey, we work on exposure."

He added EXPOSURE to his list before looking up at her with a frown. "I can see how exposure works for people, but how would you expose a town?"

"You could advertise. Glossy brochures in airports and visitor's centers. Billboards—"

He shook his head. "No good. Advertising costs money. Your client is broke."

Hallie snapped her fingers as though she just remembered. "That's right. Against my better, capitalistic nature, I've taken on a charity case."

He flashed a grin that could have melted stone. "Exactly."

"Then we go for free exposure. Facebook, blogs, you know, social media stuff." Ideas tumbled through her brain as she warmed to the topic. "I suppose we could write up a chatty article touting the reasons for visiting Village Green and submit it to a travel magazine."

"Sounds simple." He frowned. "But if we wrote an article, would anybody print it?"

"Yes. Ordinarily, I wouldn't be so certain because many of the magazines rely solely on staff writers, but I happen to have a connection at *Texas Travels*. I did some gratis work for them a while back. They owe me."

"Charity again? From the queen of capitalism?"

She had to laugh. "No way. It's referred to as a reciprocal agreement. You know—you scratch my back and I'll scratch yours."

His eyes lit with humor. "I'm familiar with the practice, but I'm not entirely sure the bank is ready to add back scratching to our services."

Something about the look he sent her caused a stirring in her chest. Hallie frowned. They'd strayed into dangerous territory. Détente or not, flirting was not an option. She made a point of checking the time on her phone. "Wow, it's late. Didn't Miss Tillie say you have a one o'clock appointment?"

Trey glanced at his watch, pulled out his wallet, and dropped a few bills on the check. When he stood to leave, she scooped up the cash and held it out to him. "Take this. I'm paying. It's my celebration."

He waved the money away. "You can buy next time."

She continued to hold out his cash. "I'm not planning on a next time."

He smiled. "I wouldn't bank on that."

As she watched him walk out of the diner, she couldn't decide if he'd just made a friendly remark or an ominous threat.

CHAPTER EIGHT

Buddy Gunther, chamber president and Trey's father, hammered his gavel on the tabletop podium set up in the back of Estelle's Diner for their regular Thursday morning meeting. "The motion to accept last month's minutes of the Village Green Chamber of Commerce passes. Let's open the floor for new business."

Lester Ainsworth shot his hand into the air. "Before we do that, I suggest we reopen last month's discussion of favorite fishing lures. Why just last week I bought me the prettiest fly—"

"Here we go again." Trey dropped his head into his hands with a muffled groan of frustration. "Sam," he whispered, nudging his friend sitting beside him. "You're a cop. Can't you do something?"

"Sorry, pal. There's no law on the books against being stupid."

Joe Wolfe, the other occupant of the table snickered. "If there was, you can be sure ol' Lester would be doing hard time."

Buddy turned in their direction. "Son, have you got something to say back there?"

Trey nodded and stood. "Yes, sir, I have. As tempting as a discussion of fishing lures sounds, I'd like to request we table it this month so we can spend some time talking about improving business."

At the table next to Trey's, Eddie Bray said in a carrying voice, "Anybody notice that's all he ever wants to talk about?"

Someone shushed Eddie. "Give him a break. He's a college graduate. You know how they like to talk about what they learned in school."

Trey's father addressed him from the podium, his expression apologetic but resolute. "I'm glad you're intent upon improving business around here, son. We all are, but the truth is we bring up the subject every month, and we've never come up with a single workable plan. I know we need to have this discussion, but I think we want to save it until we have something concrete to propose."

Trey remained standing and waited for the murmurs of agreement to die down. "I agree. In light of our past failures, I consulted with an expert. We're working with a very small population—"

"You didn't need an expert to tell you that," Eddie said. "Shoot, it's painted on the sign there at the edge of town."

Trey maintained a smile, silently counted to ten, and cleared his throat. "What I was saying is because there are so few of us, we can't expect to make any significant improvements to our economy on our own. We've got to draw new people to the area."

"How are we going to do that?" Melvin Hooper said. "Nobody ever comes to Village Green. They just move away."

"You're right, Melvin." Trey raised his voice to be heard over the talking. "And if we want to build our businesses, we're going to have to reverse that trend. We need to bring people to Village Green."

"Is your expert going to show us how to do that?"

Trey paused. His original idea had been to read the three points Hallie had given him at lunch yesterday and ask the chamber to come up with ways to implement them. As he looked around the room, he realized the futility of the plan. No matter how sincere these people were, the discussion would devolve into a fishing story swap meet in five minutes or less. What they really needed was someone with experience to guide them.

Which meant he'd have to swallow his pride and ask Hallie for help. He grimaced. He wouldn't do it if he had any other options. Desperate times called for desperate measures.

"Yes." Trey forced a smile, wondering how he was going to break the news to Hallie. "I'd like to propose we invite her to our next meeting so she can run her ideas by us."

The room erupted in chatter. He was certain Estelle's Diner hadn't seen this much excitement since the grease fire back in 1993.

A motion was made, and the group voted unanimously to invite the expert.

"How soon can she come talk with us?" his father said.

Looking down into the eager faces around him, Trey felt the full weight of his responsibility. These friends and neighbors were depending on him. And his expert.

He took a deep breath. What the heck. If Hallie was going to be mad, it may as well be for a good reason. "I move we call a special meeting of the chamber on Saturday morning. Seven o'clock. I'll bring her then. We can meet at the bank since I know Estelle's got a big breakfast crowd on the weekend."

After another unanimous vote, Buddy adjourned the meeting with a bang of his gavel.

Trey waited at the table with his friends as the other chamber members filed out. Above the din of scraping chairs and conversation, Trey heard something he'd never heard before at a chamber meeting.

He heard hope.

Joe Wolfe kicked back in his chair, stretching his long legs out in front of him and folding his arms across his chest. "So, tell us, Trey. Who is this miracle worker who is going to perform CPR on our dying town?"

Trey grinned. Though he considered Joe one of his best friends and knew him better than anyone, he realized he really didn't understand him. The son of the town drunk, Joe had fought and scraped for every ounce of success he'd achieved. As his banker, Trey knew Joe had achieved plenty. And not all of it financial. He possessed an almost legendary skill with the ladies. Young or old, he had only to turn a soulful gaze upon them, and they were putty in his hands.

But while the women couldn't seem to resist his dark good looks, Trey knew Joe faced daily all the distrust and suspicion a small town could dish out. And yet, he stayed.

"The miracle worker is Hallie Nichols."

Joe cocked a brow. "Would that be 'Let's Get It On' Janice Nichols's little sister?"

Trey nodded. "The same."

"I ran into Hallie the other day." Sam let out a low whistle. "Man, I could hardly believe it was her. She's looking mighty fine."

"Really?" Joe straightened a fraction. "Maybe I need to extend a personal welcome back to town."

Trey's stomach clenched, along with his fists. His voice flattened. "No, you don't want to do that."

"Sure, I do." Joe stopped, looking from one man to the other. He studied Trey's face for a moment. "What? You got something going on with her?"

"He had a thing for her back in high school," Sam said.

Joe snorted. "Yeah, and that was like ten years ago, right? Isn't there some kind of statute of limitations on high school things?"

"He has a point," Sam said. "Seems like ten years would make her a free agent."

Both men watched Trey, no doubt waiting for an explanation for his outburst. Unfortunately, he didn't have one. He had no idea where the sudden protectiveness came from. He rubbed a hand along the back of his neck. "You're right. She's nothing to me." Trey shrugged. "Look, forget I said anything, okay? She's fair game."

Joe and Sam exchanged a look.

"Okay, man," Joe said.

"Sure, Trey. Whatever you say."

An awkward silence stretched between the three friends. Finally, Sam pushed back from the table and stood. "I guess I need to get back to the office."

"Expecting a crime spree, officer?" Joe chuckled.

Sam grinned. "Not likely. Barring any unforeseen excitement, it's paperwork for me."

Trey stood beside him. "I need to head out too. I've got a meeting at nine I need to prep for."

"If you two are going to rush off, then there's not much reason for me to stay." Joe stretched.

"Don't you have something to do?" Sam said. "Doesn't seem right you get to sit around on your butt all day while the rest of us work. Even rich, entrepreneur types work sometimes, don't they?"

Joe laughed and stood. "Not if they can help it."

The threesome moved toward the door together.

Trey held it open for the other two. "See you Saturday."

"Yeah. You, and your expert."

Newly widowed Helen West was an attractive woman in her mid-fifties. Though she and her husband had kept mainly to themselves over the last couple of years, Trey knew they were good, godly people with a strong marriage. Helen had been devastated by Elmer's death. When she met Trey at her home that morning, he could see the shadows of grief lingering in her eyes.

"Come in, Trey." She opened the screen door for him and stepped aside for him to enter. "Can I get you something to eat?"

"No, thank you, ma'am. I just ate a big breakfast at Estelle's."

"What about some coffee then? Or tea? I think I may even have some hot chocolate somewhere."

It was clear she wouldn't be comfortable until he accepted something. "Coffee would be great. Black."

He followed her into the immaculate kitchen and, at her direction, took a seat at the round table. Helen filled two mugs of steaming coffee from a pot on the stove, carried them back to the table, and sat across from him.

"I guess you're here about the note on the farm. I know I've missed two payments." She toyed with her coffee cup. "I'm planning on making good on the note, but it seems like every time I've got enough money to pay the bank, I get another bill from the hospital."

He smiled gently and nodded. "I understand. Elmer was sick a long time, and medical care doesn't come cheap."

She continued to avoid his gaze and shook her head. "No, it doesn't. But don't worry. I'll find a way to pay it all."

He set his mug on the table and leaned in. "I'd like to help if you'd let me. We can work on the problem together."

There was a world of relief in her wounded eyes as they finally lifted to meet his. "Thank you. Yes, I could use your help."

Trey was good with money, but he was no magician. After two long hours, up to his elbows in bills and receipts, he found enough resources to pay off her debts with some to spare but not enough money to hold onto the farm.

"I really don't mind," she said when he broke the news to her. "Honestly, between the house and the land, it's too much for me to keep up. Since Elmer's gone, I feel so isolated out here. It's silly I know, but it's a little frightening to live alone. It would be a relief to be rid of the place."

After she insisted on fixing him a sandwich at noon, Trey left with the understanding he would handle the sale of her farm. When it sold, Helen could use the equity to purchase a smaller home in town. In the meantime, she could look for a job.

His mind was so full of Helen's troubles, he hadn't given much thought to his own until he climbed behind the steering wheel. Specifically, how in the world would he convince Hallie to speak to the chamber of commerce bright and early Saturday morning?

No point in putting it off. He drove past the bank and on to the Nichols's house. When he arrived, he pulled his truck into the narrow driveway behind Hallie's car and shut off the engine to do a little strategizing.

Ordinarily in a situation like this, he'd appeal to the person's sense of civic responsibility. Since Hallie admitted she was all for bulldozing the town, he didn't think civic pride would motivate her.

He bowed his head. *"Lord, it appears that in your infinite wisdom and questionable sense of humor You've decided to use Hallie, the last person I would ever willingly ask for help, to answer my prayer. I take some comfort in the fact she won't be any happier to hear about it than I am. You heard me open my big mouth this morning and promise she'd appear at the chamber meeting on Saturday. Any thoughts on how I accomplish it?"*

Five minutes later, having received no lightning bolt answer from heaven, Trey climbed out of the truck. He couldn't sit there all day. He'd just have to wing it and trust God to fill in the blanks.

The front door was open, so he called through the screen. "Anybody home?"

Mrs. Nichols answered from somewhere inside. "Come on in, Trey."

He stepped into the house, pausing to let his eyes adjust to the shadows. He crossed the living room and crouched in front of her chair so they were eye to eye. He took her hand and gave it a friendly squeeze. "How's it going?"

Mrs. Nichols sighed. "Not too well. Hallie is trying to kill me."

Hallie walked into the room behind him. A glance over his shoulder told him she was wearing a faded T-shirt and pair of worn jeans, certainly no reason to explain the sudden jump in his pulse.

"Hello, Trey." She nodded toward him and turned to her mother. "Don't say stuff like that. I'm not trying to kill you. I'm trying to help you."

Trey could tell by Hallie's weary tone of voice this was not a new argument for them. He stood. "It sounds like I've come at a bad time. Maybe I should come back later."

Hallie shook her head. "No, now's fine. What do you need?"

"I wanted to ask you something."

"Maybe you can talk to her for me. She might listen to you." Mrs. Nichols sent him a pleading glance. "Would you mind telling the exercise bully here to ease up? Remind her I am a sick woman. I'm recovering from a very serious stroke. The doctor said I could have died."

Hallie stepped around Trey to face her mother. "Mom, the exercises are the doctor's idea, not mine. He says if we don't keep using your muscles, we'll lose the mobility you gained in rehab. You don't want to be an invalid the rest of your life, do you?"

"I just don't see why you have to push me so hard." Her mother sniffled. "You can be sure Janice wouldn't abuse me this way."

Hallie opened her mouth to respond, then seemed to change her mind. She turned to Trey. "Why don't you come to the kitchen with me? I was fixing tea when I heard you come in. Mom, do you want some iced tea?"

Her response was as sulky as her expression. "No. Thank you."

Trey followed Hallie down the hall, intrigued by the feminine sway of her hips despite her rigid shoulders.

He nodded toward the living room and her mother. "Sounds like you've already put in a full day."

Hallie blew out an exasperated breath. "You don't know the half of it."

"Sit down." He crossed to the cabinets. "I remember where your mother keeps the glasses. Let me pour you some iced tea."

The fact Hallie followed his instructions without an argument was an indication of her agitation. He filled a glass and carried it to the table. "Drink up."

"Thanks. I'm sorry you had to witness our little spat."

He fixed a tea for himself and joined her at the table. "Forget it. She's been giving you a pretty hard time, huh?"

Hallie rubbed her eyes with the heels of her hands. "Don't get me started. I'm afraid once I begin talking, I won't be able to stop. You don't deserve to be burdened with my problems."

"Sometimes it helps to talk things out."

Her gaze traveled over his face as if to gauge whether he was genuinely interested or just being polite. At last, she shrugged. "She's so angry all the time. They warned me at rehab that anger and grief are part of the process of coming to terms with her stroke. Their advice was to try not to take it personally."

"Easier said than done, I imagine."

"Exactly. Especially when she makes those little remarks about Janice not treating her so badly. They hurt the worst. She seems to have forgotten Janice isn't the one who dropped everything to come here to take care of her." Her voice trailed off.

He leaned in, bracing his forearms on the table. "What can I do to help?"

She smiled and leaned back. "You've done it. The financial reports you gave me yesterday are my ticket out of here." Her face fell. "That sounds so selfish, doesn't it? I've never been so torn in my whole life. On the one hand, I can't wait to get out of here. I'm counting the seconds until I can get back to my life. On the other hand, I feel so guilty for wanting to leave. What kind of daughter would want to abandon her own mother?"

"It's not wrong to want to live your own life. You have nothing to feel guilty for."

"I just want to be a good daughter." Tears welled up and she halted a moment, as if waiting to get control before speaking. "I am a good daughter. I just want her to realize it."

He smiled. "You're a wonderful daughter. She's lucky to have you."

"Mom doesn't seem to think so."

"Then she's wrong." He smiled into brimming brown eyes that seemed to beg for reassurance. "You're doing an awesome job. She couldn't ask for better care. Even from Janice."

"That's nice to hear." She swiped at a tear with the back of her hand, took a deep breath, and pinned a bright smile on her face. "That concludes my pity party. Now, tell me why you're here. You said you needed to ask me something?"

His stomach clenched. "Yeah. I . . . uh . . . need a favor."

"After listening to me whine, I guess I owe you one. What do you need?"

Okay, Lord. This was encouraging. He relaxed a fraction. Still, it'd be best to break it to her in stages. "I need some of your marketing savvy. Actually, the town needs it. I'd like you to meet with the chamber of commerce and share your ideas with them on how to promote Village Green."

"No. Absolutely not. No way." In case he didn't get the verbal message, she shook her head while waving her hands. "You wrote them on a piece of paper, didn't you? You can tell the chamber. I feel they would be received a whole lot better if the ideas came from your mouth."

"They won't listen to me." When she shot him a disbelieving look, he nodded. "I'm serious. You're the one with the credentials. I'm just that Gunther kid who's always talking about building up business."

Hallie folded her arms and cocked a brow. "Forgive me if I have a hard time believing you can't get anyone to listen to you."

Was that a compliment? Probably not. Most likely another dig about being a Gunther. "It's true. Especially if they have a choice between me and fishing lures."

"Huh?"

"Long story." He lifted his gaze to hers. "The point is Village Green is going through a rough patch right now, but it's a good town. It's got heart. And a real sense of community." He sighed. "Unfortunately, heart and community don't sign paychecks or put food on the table."

He thought about Helen West. Her aspirations were modest. She wanted to stay in Village Green, buy a little house, and live among people she'd known most of her life. But to live in any kind of comfort with something set aside for emergencies, she'd have to find a job. And there were no jobs in Village Green.

"We need to attract people to the town." He toyed with his glass. "We need to show them it's a great place to visit, a great place to put down roots and raise a family."

"The idea being if people come to Village Green, even if it's just a visit, they'll spend money on the goods and services the local businesses provide?"

"Exactly." He nodded, smiling at her quick grasp of the situation. "Increased demand means more jobs. More jobs attract more people. More people mean more business. It's a cycle of prosperity."

She propped her chin on her hand and tapped her fingertips on her cheek. Her nails were short and painted the palest pink. "Sounds to me like you've got it all figured out."

He sighed. "If only that were true. Let's face it. I'd have to be blind not to see the problem. But finding the solution isn't so obvious." He paused. "At least it wasn't until I heard you talk about your job. It may sound crazy, but it was as if a light came on. I think your three points are the answer."

She frowned. "Let me remind you those points were designed to improve the image of an individual, not a town."

"I think they'd work for both." Palms flat on the table, he leaned in. "I believe it's worth a shot. What have we got to lose?"

She gave a short, mirthless laugh. "You, nothing. You're Trey Gunther, town golden boy. But me? Janice Nichols's little sister? If I stand in front of the chamber, I'll be chewed up and spit out. You heard them at Estelle's. I'm like a bug under a microscope wherever I go. It's mortifying. It's bad enough knowing they're studying me, but it's worse to know they'll want to point out all of my shortcomings, in painful detail, to anyone who will listen."

She was probably correct. By appearing before the chamber, she'd be the target of undeserved criticism. It was a crummy thing to ask of her.

But if she didn't meet with them, they'd never hear and consider her ideas. Nothing would change. Village Green's economy would remain in the tank. Helen West wouldn't be able to find work.

He lowered his head, studied his hands. "I'm sorry, Hallie. Truly. I wouldn't ask you to do this if it wasn't so important. Not just to me. To the community. I don't think I'm exaggerating to say the future of the town could be riding on this." He blew out a breath before lifting his gaze to meet hers. "I need you."

She peered at him closely before sighing in what sounded like resignation. "When is the next chamber of commerce meeting?"

Hope flooded him. Unfortunately, there was still one more hurdle to clear. One *big* hurdle.

"You're slated to speak on Saturday." He blurted out the words in an undignified rush.

"At 7:00 a.m."

"Saturday?" Her eyes flew wide open. Though to her credit, she didn't scream like he'd half expected her to. "Did you say Saturday?" Her voice climbed an octave. "As in the day after tomorrow?"

He dipped his head slightly in a guilty sort of nod.

"At seven o'clock in the morning?" By now her voice was an incredulous squeak. "Hours before normal people are waking up on the weekend?"

He nodded again.

"And you've already told them I'll be there?" Her tone normalized, became accusatory. She glared at him. "You committed me without asking?"

His third nod made him feel like the stupid dog with the bobbing head Miss Tillie kept in the back window of her car. "Yes."

"You're pretty sure of yourself, aren't you?"

He shook his head. He'd never been less sure in his life. "Just desperate."

She regarded him with a long, penetrating look, then her expression turned shrewd. "How desperate?"

Trey was sweating now. Really? He swallows his pride to ask for help, and she's giving him a hard time? His town is teetering on the brink of extinction, and she wants to negotiate? They were so close. He needed her commitment. He'd promised her to the chamber. They were expecting her. He racked his brain for any kind of bargaining chip. What did he have that she wanted?

"Desperate enough that if you'll do this for me, I . . . uh . . . I won't ask you to meet with me about your expenditures for your mom."

Her face lit up. "Really?"

He frowned. She didn't have to look so pleased. "Absolutely."

"Wait a minute. I thought we had to meet." She narrowed her eyes. "Something about upholding the sacred vows you made to my dad."

He chose to ignore the sarcasm. And the question. "I told you I'm desperate."

She paused, turning the glass of tea in her hands, apparently weighing her dread of standing in front of the chamber versus meeting weekly with him.

Seconds ticked by. He kneaded the muscles in the back of his neck. So much was riding on this. His chair creaked when he leaned forward. "Well, what do you think? Will you do it?"

Slowly, she lifted her gaze to his. "Yeah. I'll be there."

CHAPTER NINE

Saturday morning at ten minutes to seven, every parking space in front of the bank was taken, an assortment of pickup trucks slanted into each spot, forcing Hallie to drive another block to find an open space. Big crowd. She refused to dwell on the horrific thought. She pulled in front of one of the many boarded-up stores lining the street and shut off the engine.

She glanced through the windshield and grimaced. Graying plywood covered the showroom windows of the long-abandoned catalog store. A tattered For Sale or Rent sign hung crookedly from a lone nail.

Village Green would make a perfect set for some apocalyptic movie. It needed only a pack of wandering zombies to complete the bleak scenario. What suggestion did she have to offer to turn this around? What could she possibly say? She gathered her leather tote from the passenger seat and climbed out of the car, locking the door more out of habit than necessity.

The deteriorating sidewalk, though not as bad as the one circling the Green, provided a real challenge to the black heels she wore. She stepped gingerly around the cracks, careful to protect the costly shoes from scuffs. She'd paid a fortune for them a year ago, her first real splurge when she'd started her own business. She reasoned the expense was completely justified. After all, an image specialist couldn't wear just any old shoes.

The pair more than paid for themselves in the confidence boost they provided. The moment she slipped her feet into the gleaming leather, she transformed from self-conscious Hallie Nichols to Superwoman, sans the spandex.

Her heels clicked on the pavement as she hurried toward the bank. She'd need superpowers and more to get through this morning's meeting.

Why had she agreed to do this? Hallie had asked herself the question a dozen times since Trey left her mother's house on Thursday. She'd rather have a root canal without anesthesia in front of a hundred rolling cameras on live TV than face the chamber of commerce. Not only did she have nothing to offer them, even if she had the solution to their problems, they wouldn't listen to her. She'd consider herself lucky if they didn't laugh her from the podium.

The front door of the bank swung open, and Trey stepped out. He wore a crisp blue button-down shirt, sleeves rolled to his forearms, and a pair of well-worn jeans. A wide smile stretched across his impossibly handsome face when he waved.

This was all his fault.

The blame for the impending debacle lay entirely at his loafer-shod feet. She was here at the crack of dawn, on a doomed mission of mercy, because he'd caught her at a weak moment and played on her sympathies.

Sure, he'd handed her a nice concession by letting her off the hook for the weekly financial meetings. And she'd be lying to say it wouldn't be great to get him out of her hair once and for all. But that wasn't why she was up before the sun this morning.

Closing the distance between them, she studied him. He loved this miserable town. His devotion to Village Green and its inhabitants showed in the light in his eyes, the conviction in his voice, even his posture. And while she didn't share his sentiment, she hadn't been able to resist the rare vulnerability she'd seen in his face or the plea in his proud voice. I need you.

Self-sufficient Trey had asked her for help. So here she was.

Waving, he stepped aside for her to enter. "Thanks for coming."

"I didn't know I had a choice."

He chuckled. "To be honest, I figured the odds were no better than fifty-fifty you'd show up."

He swung the heavy door closed and locked it behind them with a decisive thunk, sealing her fate. He signaled her to follow him.

As they passed through the lobby, Hallie heard voices coming from the interior of the building. A lot of voices. "I'm still pretty sure it's a bad idea."

He must have heard the trepidation in her tone. He stopped and looked down at her, compassion in his eyes. "Nervous?"

"A little." She lied. She was *a lot* nervous. And mildly nauseated.

"Don't be." He took her clammy hand in his cool one and gave it a quick reassuring squeeze before releasing it. "Piece of cake."

She smoothed her dress, a slim knee-length splash of fire engine red, before following Trey into the bank conference room. She depended on the dress to say confidence, poise, and competence, all the things she wasn't feeling.

When she entered the paneled room, silence fell as a dozen pairs of eyes homed in on her like heat-seeking missiles. Her stomach dipped in a slow greasy slide. Seated along one side of the rectangular table and in chairs lined against the wall were the "movers and shakers" of Village Green, if you could use the term for a town of less than a thousand where the major cultural event of the week was the changing of the movie posters at the Grocery Giant's video rental desk.

She swallowed hard. She'd grown up under the critical eye of these people. They'd never take her seriously.

Trey's father was seated at the far end of the table. A handsome man in his early sixties, he smiled, stood, and crossed the room to greet her. He shook her hand warmly. "We appreciate you coming to speak to us this morning. Trey says you've got some important things to share with us."

Her uneasy stomach knotted. Her lips trembled as she smiled. "Thank you for inviting me."

"Everybody's here," Trey said. "We can start whenever you're ready."

Hallie took a deep breath for courage. *I can do this.* She fisted her hands at her sides. "Let's go."

Trey's father called the meeting to order, thanked Mayor John Sellers and his council members for joining them, then returned to his seat. Hallie and Trey remained standing at the front of the room. After Pastor Dale led the group in a quick prayer, Trey introduced Hallie.

Eddie Bray raised his hand. "I thought you said you were bringing in an expert. That's just the youngest Nichols girl."

Hallie's face flamed. It was worse than she'd imagined, and she hadn't spoken a single word. Her heart sank into her Superwoman shoes.

Trey's smile never faltered when he placed a supportive hand on her shoulder. "Hallie is a professional image consultant and the owner of a very successful public relations company in Fort Worth. She has graciously offered to share her valuable expertise and insight with us. I'm looking forward to hearing what she has to say."

She thanked him for his kind introduction and waited until he took his seat halfway down the table before addressing the assembly.

"Trey asked me to speak to you this morning about creating a strategy for improving the image of Village Green."

"Seems pretty presumptuous for a little gal to be criticizing her hometown when she's been gone for the better part of her life," Eddie whispered loudly to Chet Wilke.

"Shh," Chet whispered back, but loud enough for all to hear. "For crying out loud, give the girl a chance to talk."

Eddie's words hung over the room like a dark cloud. However tempting, Hallie knew ignoring them wouldn't make them go away. "Mr. Bray has a valid point. It would be presumptuous of me to criticize Village Green." She paused, waiting until every eye was on her. "But I haven't come to criticize. I've come to offer help. I think we can all agree there is room for improvement in even the best of places. And sometimes being away from a situation allows the observer to gain a new perspective. I'd like to share my perspective with you today."

She earned several half-hearted nods from the group and a wink from Trey. She turned to the graph paper flip chart set up on an easel behind her. This would be so much easier if this was PowerPoint. Instead, she picked up the black marker from the tray and wrote GOALS/OBJECTIVES at the top of the page. The squeak of the marker on paper was the only sound in the room, if you didn't count the wild hammering of her heart against her ribcage.

"She's got real nice handwriting," Eddie allowed, perhaps trying to make up for his earlier rudeness.

Hallie faced her audience. "It's critical at the beginning of any project to identify the desired outcome. So, let's start here." She pointed to the words she'd written. "What are our goals? What is it we want to accomplish?"

A dozen blank faces stared back at her. It was abundantly clear from their expressions and crossed arms they were not onboard with the exercise or Hallie. She refused to squirm or hunch her shoulders in defeat. By sheer force of will, she stood tall, the picture of relaxed poise.

A single bead of perspiration trickled down her spine.

"We want to draw people and businesses to Village Green," Trey called out after an uncomfortable silence.

She flashed him a smile of gratitude. "Good." She wrote DRAW BUSINESS AND PEOPLE TO VILLAGE GREEN under the heading. She faced the group with an encouraging smile. "What other goals do we have?"

Silence. Everyone continued to stare. Unmoving. Waiting.

After allowing a moment or two for someone, *anyone*, to offer a suggestion, Hallie pointed to the only entry on the paper. "This is an excellent start. Let's move on and ask ourselves what image we want Village Green to project."

She smiled bravely into the faces watching her, nodding in an attempt to gain a response. Her smile was so wide her cheeks hurt. Nothing. She heard the air conditioner cycle on overhead. "Anybody?"

"I think we want a small-town, family-oriented feeling."

"That's good. Thank you, Trey." More nods. More smiles. "Anyone else?"

More nothing. She lifted the marker to the paper and eyed the group from over her shoulder. "Does that mean everyone agrees with Trey's suggestion?"

This time a few heads nodded. She wrote it on the paper. "What about welcoming? Do we want people to feel welcome in Village Green?"

A couple more nods. She wrote WELCOMING under SMALL TOWN, FAMILY ORIENTED. Confident she couldn't pry any more input from the participants, she wrote her next heading, APPEARANCE, on the page.

"Now, for this section, I'm going to ask you all to imagine you are strangers coming to Village Green for the first time. I'd like you to close your eyes and pretend you are driving down the highway and about to turn onto Main Street."

"Are we coming in from the north or south?" Eddie asked, his eyes squeezed tightly shut.

Hallie smiled. "North. Now everyone try to picture Village Green in your mind." She looked around the room for a volunteer, someone who was likely to contribute something sensible. "Pastor Dale, what do you see?"

"I see the sign for Village Green."

"Excellent. That's a great place to start. Now tell me, does the sign support our welcoming, small-town, family-oriented image?"

His eyes still closed, he scrunched up his face. "No, not really. Actually, it looks a little tired, like it could use a fresh coat of paint."

"It's got all kinda weeds growing up over it," Chet chimed in. "Last couple times I drove past it I thought I needed to take a clipper to all those vines."

It was as if a dam broke. Suddenly, everyone had something to say. Hallie wrote at top speed to keep up with the flood of suggestions tossed out. She'd covered all of one large page and half of the next before they ran out of ideas.

"Let me recap what we've come up with so far." Hallie read off the list of needed improvements which covered everything from repainting the city limits sign to repairing the sidewalks and the one-hundred-year-old wrought iron fence surrounding the Green.

"I can see where you're going here." Estelle from the diner had contributed lots of useful ideas and was obviously excited about the possibilities. "We need to pretty things up if we're going to look welcoming. But what happens once we get the place cleaned up? How do we get people to come see what we've done?"

"Good question. And that leads us to our third and final step." Hallie flipped to a new page and wrote EXPOSURE. "After we feel we have the town polished up to our satisfaction, we advertise. Since we don't have a budget for advertising, we improvise." She took a step toward the group. "Social media is an excellent means of getting the word out at no cost. The city can construct a website. And I have a connection at *Texas Travels*, a monthly magazine that features different points of interest within the state in each issue. If you like, I'd be happy to submit an article to them about Village Green. The publicity will encourage tourists to visit the city."

"I think we should come up with a town motto," Mr. Gunther suggested. "Lots of places have them. We could paint it on the city limits sign. If it were catchy enough, folks driving by might be tempted to stop by and take a look."

Hallie turned to write MOTTO on the board. "A motto is a great idea. It's a way to solidify our brand in the minds of the public."

"Who's gonna come up with the motto?" Eddie scratched his chin. "You know, I'm pretty good at stuff like that."

Hallie rushed in before he could appoint himself. "The chamber of commerce could sponsor a town motto contest. It would give everyone a chance to participate. You could ask for motto suggestions and the chamber could pick their top ten choices from the submissions and type them up on a ballot. You can distribute ballot boxes around town and let people vote for their favorite."

Everyone talked at once. They might be slow to embrace change, but once they were hooked, it'd be tough to find a more enthusiastic crowd.

"I think we need to establish some sort of timetable." Trey stood to be heard. "Let's figure out a reasonable amount of time to make the repairs and improvements and then set a deadline for them to be completed."

Hallie nodded. "He's right. We could tie the announcement of the winner of the motto contest to the completion of the improvements."

Buddy Gunther stood and rapped the table with his gavel. "Let's have some order, please."

The group quieted.

"I believe we're on to something here." Buddy pointed toward the flip chart. "I know you'll all agree with me that Hallie's plan to polish up our town has given us a lot to think about. I'd like to call for a vote on whether we want to tackle a revitalization program. All in favor?"

Every person in the room shot up a hand with gratifying speed.

"That settles it." Buddy smiled warmly at her. "Let's give Hallie a round of applause to thank her for sharing her ideas with us today."

She'd never heard a sweeter sound than the applause and approval from the same people whose stinging criticism in the past still had the power to wound her. After the clapping faded, her gaze swept the assembled group. "It has been my pleasure. I wish you all the best. I know you will be very successful."

She sat in the empty chair at the head of the table with an enormous sense of relief. The ordeal was over. She'd survived it without a single bruise. It was nice to be appreciated, and even nicer to return the leadership of the meeting to Mr. Gunther. This was his baby, not hers.

Buddy raised his hands for quiet. "Before we leave, I propose we divide into committees, with each group taking responsibility for one part of our revitalization project. Trey and Hallie can serve as our coleaders."

Hallie and Trey shared a look of alarm across the table and spoke at once, talking over each other in their panic.

"I can't—"

"She can't—"

"I'm leaving—"

"She's leaving—"

Buddy smiled. "We understand Hallie has a job in Fort Worth. But as a professional, she knows she can't drop a project of this magnitude in our laps. We will need her guidance and expertise to see it to completion."

Hallie shook her head and tried for a pleasant but firm tone of voice. "Mr. Gunther, I have a company to run. I have clients depending on me. I am only going to be in Village Green long enough to arrange care for my mother, then I'm leaving."

His smile never wavered. "Then I guess we'll just have to work fast."

"But—"

He frowned. "Hallie, don't you have enough faith in your plan to want to see it through?"

All eyes zeroed in on Hallie. Watching. Waiting.

Talk about pressure. Hallie felt as though she was sitting on the witness stand, facing a hostile jury. Was it her imagination or did she see doubt in the faces which reflected admiration and confidence just moments ago?

"Little Hallie is mighty young to be heading up an important project like this," Eddie said. "I think we can all agree she's got some fine ideas, but she doesn't have the experience needed to get the job done."

Her heart sank when several heads bobbed in agreement. The verdict was in. Again, Hallie Nichols had been found guilty. She didn't measure up. These people, the ones who had known her the better part of her life, didn't think she could do the job.

She pushed to her feet without conscious thought. "Mr. Gunther, I have complete faith in my plan." She made a slow, deliberate scan of the faces positioned around the table, carefully meeting each set of eyes before moving on to the next. "So much faith, in fact, that if we can set a reasonable timetable for completing the work, I will accept coleadership of the project."

CHAPTER TEN

Trey moved around the now-empty conference room, gathering papers and cups left on the table and pushing in the chairs. Hallie had remained behind with him after the meeting dismissed and sat by the door. "Why in the world did you let my father manipulate you into taking responsibility for the revitalization?"

The wide-eyed look on her face said she was as shocked as he was. "Probably for the same reason you did."

Trey tossed the trash in the waste basket. "Wrong. I live here. It's my town. It's my responsibility. I'm obligated to help out. You're not. You said it yourself. You're just passing through."

"Maybe I wanted to do a good deed for my hometown. You know, civic duty and all that."

He snorted. "Yeah, right. A few days ago the only humane solution for Village Green was to bulldoze the place, and suddenly today you want to save it?"

She lifted her chin. "It's a woman's prerogative to change her mind."

As he continued to stare at her in blatant disbelief, her veneer of bravado evaporated, and her slender shoulders drooped. "Fine, I haven't changed my mind. I don't know why I let him bully me into accepting. Chalk it up to temporary insanity."

Trey scrubbed a hand over his face. "You're stuck now. You know that, right? You couldn't back out if you wanted to." He huffed out a breath. "I'm sorry. I know you're eager to get home. We have no choice but to make the best of a bad situation. I'm pretty confident the committees can handle the bulk of the work, so we'll basically need to set up the plan and supervise the implementation."

A sense of urgency had him glancing at his watch. "Do you have time to grab breakfast at Estelle's? We can draft a roughed-out strategy for how we're going to accomplish all this."

Hallie's hair swept the top of her shoulders when she shook her head. "No, I'm sorry. I can't. I've been away too long already. I worry Mom will fall while I'm gone."

"I understand." And he did. She didn't owe him anything. She'd generously spent her morning with him and the chamber despite her dislike of both. She'd earned a break. And yet . . .

This morning's meeting filled him with energy that needed an outlet. With a potential solution in sight, he was past ready to dig in and get things rolling.

"It's just that I think we need to get started with our part. People will be looking to us for direction, and I want to be sure you and I are on the same page."

She caught her bottom lip in her teeth. "Tell you what, I need to get back to the house. Why don't you come with me? I can fix us something to eat while we brainstorm."

Her offer brought a smile of surprise to his lips. "Babysitting and brainstorming." He nodded. "That'll work. If you want to head out, I'll lock up here. I'll join you at your mom's place in ten minutes."

"Sounds good." Hallie pointed to the flip chart propped on the easel. "We're going to want those notes."

"I'll bring them along."

Trey's thoughts circled crazily as he made the short drive to the Nichols's and parked in the driveway. He hadn't seen this coming. A handful of scenarios had played through his mind prior to the meeting, but not one featured him and Hallie teaming up to save the town.

He chuckled as he gathered the flip chart from the backseat of his truck and headed across the lawn to the stairs. Talk about irony. The woman least interested in the survival of the town was the one charged with making it happen, while partnered with the man she'd do anything to avoid.

He rapped on the screen door.

Mrs. Nichols beamed at him from her chair. "Come in. It's becoming a regular thing to see you around here."

"Yes, ma'am." He stepped inside and, after laying the chart on the coffee table, crossed the room to take her hand in greeting. "And it looks like it's going to become a daily occurrence, at least for a while. Did Hallie tell you she and I are cochairing a revitalization project for the town?"

"I haven't had time." Hallie called from the kitchen. "Why don't you two come in here with me, and we can talk while I make breakfast."

Trey waited as Mrs. Nichols levered herself from her chair in painstaking degrees. He walked by her side as he'd seen Hallie do while the older woman slowly made her way down the hall to the kitchen. He now understood why Hallie was so worried about her falling. The woman teetered precariously with every step. It was a relief to finally pull out a chair for her at the table and help her get settled.

"I'm making bacon and scrambled eggs." Hallie stood barefoot in front of a pan of bacon already sizzling on the stove.

She'd stashed the sexy heels she'd worn to the meeting by the door and slipped a faded apron over her dress. The homey, domestic look was a far cry from the jaw-dropping woman who showed up at the bank this morning. She'd said she was nervous, but he'd never have guessed it by looking at her. The sophisticated red dress and sleek shoes declared her a woman with everything under control. "We've also got blueberry muffins that Sarah Danson brought by yesterday."

He took the seat next to her mother. "Sounds like a feast."

"I hope you're hungry." Hallie delivered a napkin-lined basket of muffins to the table.

"Starved."

"Me too." She opened the refrigerator and pulled out a carton of eggs. "Must be a reaction to all the nerves from this morning. The only thing I ate before the meeting was a fistful of antacids."

Mrs. Nichols selected a muffin from the basket. "So how did your speech go?"

"Hallie was brilliant." Trey picked up a muffin and peeled off the paper. "She faced down a tough crowd and had them eating out of her hand by the end of the meeting."

"Thanks to you." Hallie sent him a smile while breaking eggs into a mixing bowl. "If you hadn't offered suggestions to get us started, I'd still be standing there with a stupid smile on my face and a marker in my hand."

He could laugh about it now, though at the time he'd wanted to weep with frustration. "That was intense, wasn't it?"

She grimaced. "I'll say. It was so quiet I'm sure every person in the room could hear my heart pounding."

"Mine too. I felt like I was having a heart attack. Until that moment, I didn't realize the chamber was capable of intimidation. And I had no idea they were capable of silence."

"But once they got started talking, I couldn't shut them up. It was fun to see them get excited." Hallie turned her attention to the bowl of eggs and whipped them with a wire whisk.

Mrs. Nichols folded her arms like a bad-tempered child and huffed. "I'm hoping one of you will be kind enough to explain to me what it is you're talking about."

"I'm sorry." Trey shifted in his seat to focus his attention on her. "As you know, this morning Hallie met with the chamber of commerce and Mayor Sellers to suggest ways to attract business to our town. She was so inspiring that by the conclusion of the meeting the group voted unanimously to adopt her plan, and they appointed us to lead it."

"Well, congratulations." She smiled at Trey before leveling a scowl on her daughter. "I'm surprised you agreed to do it, Hallie, since all you can talk about is getting back to Fort Worth." Sulky undertones of hurt and disapproval tinged her voice.

He silently applauded Hallie's restraint in refusing to take the bait. She maintained an unruffled smile as she carefully poured the eggs into a waiting skillet. "It was a surprise to me too. I'd forgotten just how persuasive Buddy Gunther can be. But I do have a company to run. So, I'm hoping once Trey and I get things rolling, I'll be able to handle my part of the revitalization remotely from Fort Worth."

Trey shrugged. "I don't see why you couldn't. But I think you'll want to be here for the festival."

Mrs. Nichols brightened. "Festival?"

Hallie looked up from the stove to narrow her eyes at him. "What festival?"

"Sounds great, right?" He lifted his palms to silence the argument he saw coming. "Just hear me out. While you were speaking this morning, I kept thinking we need something to tie it all together once the revitalization is complete. You know, some sort of event to cap off the work, to showcase the efforts, and to celebrate the accomplishment."

The look on Hallie's face said she didn't share his vision. "I don't know. . . . A festival sounds pretty ambitious."

"Not really. Honestly, I'm thinking small, you know, like a local fair. I picture a string of multicolored pennants flying over a church ladies' food booth and a couple of games for the kids."

"It sounds lovely," Mrs. Nichols said. "It's been years since we've done anything like that in Village Green."

Hallie finished cooking in silence, presumably listening while he and her mother discussed the potential merits of his plan. She delivered a plate of bacon and a bowl of eggs to the table and joined them.

After the blessing, she served her mother. "I suppose if we kept it small . . ."

Trey accepted the spoon from her and scooped eggs onto his plate. "Absolutely. An hour or two of food and a couple activities, and we're done. I only chose the word festival because it sounds important." He grinned. "Some of the PR stuff you've been talking must have rubbed off on me."

He paused to consider the implication. He had let Hallie influence him. In a moment of desperation, he'd suspended his decade old resentment of her long enough to listen to what she had to say. Their past didn't seem to matter anymore. They made a lousy couple, but he felt in his bones they'd make an unstoppable team.

CHAPTER ELEVEN

Trey pulled into the church parking lot and stopped in his customary spot, the farthest point from the sidewalk leading to the sanctuary. He'd watched the small congregation age over the years and realized he needed to leave the closer places for the growing number of members who relied on walkers and canes. He glanced across the adjacent lot to the parsonage. The lights were still on in the front windows. Pastor Dale must be running through his sermon one more time before walking over to the church. Trey knew it was his turn to start the coffee then.

He grabbed the loaded folders from the passenger seat and climbed out of the truck. Balancing the papers in one hand, he fished the ring of keys from his pocket, separated the church key from the others, and unlocked the door leading into the Sunday school wing. Inside, he completed his usual Sunday morning circuit on his way to the kitchen, stepping into classrooms, flipping on overhead lights, and ensuring chairs and tables were set up in readiness for today's gathering.

He held his breath when he rounded the corner to his last stop, the kitchen. Yes! He pumped a fist in the air. The two stainless coffee urns were perched on the counter, clean and ready to be filled and switched on. He hated it when he found them sitting in the sink, meaning the Wednesday night Bible study had run over and nobody wanted to stay late to wash out the coffee pots. Not that he blamed them. He couldn't decide which was worse, washing the behemoth dispensers or trying to reassemble the surprisingly complex mechanism once they were clean. No matter. Today, he'd been spared.

He hummed tunelessly as he measured out the coffee, regular and decaf, and lugged the urns to the sink to fill them with water. They were a nightmare to clean and took a while to brew, but the old pots still made a delicious cup of coffee. After setting out cups and the wicker tray with sweetener and creamer on the countertop next to the now-percolating urns, he glanced at his watch. He had time to spend a few moments in the sanctuary before Pastor Dale joined him for their morning cup of coffee.

He walked down a short hall and entered the antechamber that opened into the front of the church. When he passed through the small, oak-paneled room, he remembered the times he'd stood there, huddled with a handful of tuxedo-clad friends, waiting for their cue from the organist. He thought of the few people of marriageable age remaining in Village Green. Definitely no weddings in the foreseeable future.

Kind of a dismal thought.

Trey stepped through the door into the sanctuary, stopped, and breathed deeply. The air smelled of history and holiness. The wood-frame church was over a hundred years old and spartan by today's plush standards, but the simplicity of the sanctuary never failed to fill him with a sense of God's presence. This morning, beams of light filtered through the richly colored stained glass windows, painting pools of color on the pews and polished floor.

His footfalls whispered along the age-smoothed planks as he walked to the center aisle and sat on the first pew. Arms propped on his thighs, he gazed up at the altar, hand-carved oak draped with an embroidered linen cloth and dressed with two tall vases of pink and white flowers from Mrs. Piermont's backyard. Beyond it, a simple wooden cross hung on the wall.

Gratitude washed over him. Here, in the quiet of the morning, he wasn't martyred in a town time forgot. Instead, he was privileged to share the legacy of the generations before him.

"I thought I'd find you here," Pastor Dale called through the open door. "Are you and the Lord conducting private business? If so, I can fix my cup of coffee, and you can join me when you're done."

"No. We're good." Trey stood and glanced up at the cross again. "It's just such a great spot to start the day."

The pastor nodded. "None better." He took a moment to scan the room. "This sanctuary is one of the things I'll miss most when I'm gone."

"What gone?" Trey smiled, walked to the older man, and took his hand in a firm handshake. "You're not going anywhere."

"You don't think an old man should retire?"

They'd been through this dozens of times before. Trey tried not to worry, but the topic seemed to come up more frequently of late. He didn't know what he'd do if his dear friend and trusted pastor actually left. "Sure, and when you're old you can retire. I'll even throw you a party."

Pastor Dale held the door for Trey, and the two of them walked side by side to the kitchen. "I'm seventy-eight, son. You probably ought to think about ordering the cake."

"No way. You're still in your prime. Besides, who'd shepherd this flock if you retired?"

"You've got a point. Tough to attract a pastor with a congregation this size. And with half the members nearly as old as I am, well, there may come a time there won't be a flock to lead."

They arrived at the coffee urns, now the source of tantalizing aroma, and Trey grabbed two Styrofoam cups, handing one to his friend. "Weren't you listening at the meeting yesterday? Things are about to change. We're going to clean up the town, do a little promoting, and the whole world is going to beat a path to our door."

Dale chuckled and filled his cup from the pot with the regular stuff. "That's not quite the way I remember it."

Trey poured his coffee and added sugar before heading to a nearby circle of gray metal folding chairs and sat. "Okay, I admit it. I may have put a bit of an optimistic spin on it."

"Of course, you did." Pastor Dale joined him, balancing his coffee in one hand, and turned one of the folding chairs so he and Trey would be facing each other. "Optimism is your middle name."

"Or foolhardy."

Dale shook his head and sat. "Nothing foolish about it. Optimism is a rare and beautiful gift. The ability to look for the best, hope for the best, and expect the best is one of the finest qualities a man can possess. You've had it all your life." He smiled. "Even as a little boy, you believed the sun always shone on you."

"How could I not? I've lived a blessed life."

"Yes and no. Your family has means, certainly, and you've never known hunger or want, but you've also shouldered enormous responsibilities. Challenges that would have caused a lesser man to become negative and bitter."

Trey shrugged. "I just do what I have to."

Dale's gaze locked with his. "But you don't have to. The survival of Village Green doesn't rest on you. Sometimes I worry that Gunther mindset of yours makes you think you have to have all the answers. That it's up to you and you alone to get this town back on its feet."

Trey winced as the remark struck uncomfortably close to home.

Dale smiled. "I admit I was pleasantly surprised to see you were willing to ask for help."

Trey lowered his eyes. "I didn't want to. And certainly not from Hallie."

The pastor chuckled. "I'm proud of you for swallowing your pride. I pray this revitalization project will be a roaring success."

"From your mouth to God's ear." Trey shot him a smile. "I'm hopeful. Hallie brought us a solid plan."

"Yes, she did." Dale nodded. "I must say, I was impressed by Hallie."

"Yeah, she really stepped up to the plate."

"She did indeed." Dale sipped his coffee. "I admit I wouldn't have expected her to champion the cause of Village Green. She never made a secret of her feelings for the town. As I recall, she left here right out of high school a deeply wounded young woman."

Trey shrugged. "I don't know about wounded. I think she bailed out before she got trapped. One more rat fleeing a sinking ship."

The pastor considered him from beneath bushy white brows. "I suppose it's possible. You two were quite an item back then. You probably knew her better than most."

"At the time I would have agreed with you, but in hindsight I realize I didn't know her at all. I was gullible enough to think she was really into all of this—turns out she was just biding her time until she could make her escape."

"That had to hurt."

Trey studied his coffee cup while he revisited the painful memory for the second time in a week. "It felt like the worst kind of betrayal. I honestly thought she lo—er, I thought she was in it with me for the long haul." He dragged his focus back to Dale. "I don't know why disloyalty cuts the deepest."

Dale eyed him over the top of his cup. "And yet she agreed to help you with this project."

"I wouldn't be looking for altruism if I were you. You heard my dad at the meeting. He backed her into a corner. She's helping me only because there was no way she could turn him down and save face."

Pastor Dale cocked a brow. "Where is that famed Gunther optimism now?"

Trey toasted him with his coffee cup. "Remember, I'm an optimist, not stupid."

CHAPTER TWELVE

Hallie delivered her mother to her Sunday school class, settling her into the circle of chairs between fawning friends, before heading out to the fellowship hall to find Trey. After their brainstorming session yesterday, his assignment had been to call the pastor to secure permission to set up an informational table somewhere in the church.

She located Trey and the pastor in an animated conversation with a cluster of people by the coffee station. She walked slowly to give Trey time to notice her approach and break from the group to save her from the embarrassment of barging in.

Unfortunately, his attention was fully engaged on his companions. She took a deep breath and approached the edge of the circle. "Good morning."

"Good morning to you." Trey's father clapped a hand on her shoulder and drew her into the group. "Here she is folks—the woman of the hour."

The mayor smiled broadly. "Hello, Hallie. Didn't get to tell you what a great job you did Saturday. You turned that group on their ear."

Estelle from the diner lifted her Styrofoam cup in a salute. "Nothing short of miraculous."

Hallie shook her head. "Oh, no. It was just—"

"It was miraculous," Estelle insisted, looking to the others for confirmation. "Trust me. Anytime the chamber gets together and the discussion doesn't deteriorate into a squabble over fishing, it's a bona fide miracle. Right up there with parting the Red Sea."

Hallie couldn't help but laugh with them. "I'm glad I could help out. I didn't mean to interrupt you all. Trey, if you will point me in the direction of our stuff, I can get it set up."

"Let me help you." He turned to address the group. "If you will excuse us, we'll get to work. Dad, I'm ducking out of class today."

Buddy Gunther smiled. "I guess I'll make it an excused absence since it's for a good cause."

While the others dispersed, Pastor Dale remained. "Trey, why don't you grab one of the extra folding tables from the custodian's closet. I'll show Hallie where we decided to place it."

Surprised, but pleased with his offered company, Hallie waited for him to lead the way.

"It's nice outside this morning. We can take the scenic route." Pastor Dale walked beside her, waiting until they were out of earshot of the others before speaking. "I wanted a private moment to tell you how very proud I am of you."

Smiling, she nodded. "Thank you. I really enjoy public relations, so it was no big deal."

He shook his white head and opened the door for her to step outside. "Your public relations skills are impressive, certainly, but that's not what I was talking about. I was referring to the forgiveness you've extended to our community."

Forgiveness? She waited on the sidewalk for him to pull the door closed and join her. "I'm sorry?"

They fell into step together, heading around the side of the church in the direction of the front door. Since Sunday school had now begun, they had the shrub-lined walkway to themselves.

"One of the inevitable results of aging is slowing down, and while my body exhibits every bit of its seventy-eight years, my mind and memory remain blessedly sharp." He tapped the side of his head. "For instance, I remember the day you left for college as though it were yesterday."

She nodded. Her own memory of what she'd dubbed emancipation day was crystal clear. Her new car, the shiny silver compact she'd received for graduation, was loaded to capacity with clothes, bedding, toiletries, and plastic totes crammed with all the necessities to make a dorm a home. Her parents' car was piled high with the overflow. She and her dad were standing in the driveway, finalizing their route plans, when Pastor Dale pulled in behind them. He'd hopped out of the car, waving a brightly decorated gift bag with goodies his wife had packed for Hallie.

"I was running late that morning and nearly missed your send-off."

Hallie smiled at the memory of his uncharacteristically harried, red face and slightly disheveled appearance that morning. He'd looked more like a mad scientist than a gentle pastor. "I remember the snickerdoodles were still warm when you delivered them."

"My Bettie knew you particularly loved her cookies." His smile grew dreamy as it did whenever he spoke of his late wife. "She insisted no one was going anywhere until she packed you a fresh batch."

After a pause, his expression cleared. "You and I took a minute to pray while your mom and dad closed up the house. When we finished, you looked at me and said you wouldn't be back. You said you were done with Village Green. You were going to find someplace where you mattered."

Hallie nodded. She didn't know what caused her to speak so freely that day. Something he'd said in the prayer about new beginnings must have lanced the festering wound in her heart and triggered the confession. She could still see the look of bewilderment on his face when the words sprang from her mouth, hot and messy like her pent-up emotions.

"I was stunned. Of course, by then your parents joined us, and there was no more time to speak privately." He shook his head. "As I watched you drive away, I wondered how I could have failed, how we all could have failed to communicate to such a precious young lady how very valuable she was? I knew your sister, Janice, was always in the spotlight, but I'd foolishly believed you were okay with that arrangement. You'd always been shy, and I guess I'd convinced myself you were more comfortable with the focus directed on her. Until that moment, when I heard the profound hurt in your voice, I never realized the damage our short-sightedness had done."

She stopped and faced him. "So that's why you and Miss Bettie sent me a card every single month I was away at school that always ended with the P.S. 'You matter more than you know.' I'd make a special trip to the mailbox about the time I knew the next one would be coming. I looked forward to them every month."

The statement earned her a slight smile as his blue eyes searched her face. "I always wondered if we should have done more. I suppose I tried to console myself that with time you would forget the hurts and realize how special you were."

"The cards helped."

They resumed walking and he said, "Too little, too late. And, true to your word, you didn't come back. You made a visit now and then, of course, but only short ones with a specific purpose, and then you were gone again. Do you know I've carried the guilt of my blindness toward your situation all these years? I don't think even I realized the depth of it until I heard you speak on Saturday. There you stood, in front of the same people who'd let you believe you weren't enough—the people who didn't deserve your kindness and effort, and yet you gave unselfishly of both time and talent to help us out of our mess." He lifted his eyes to meet hers. "The extraordinary forgiveness you've shown us is beyond humbling. And I'm very proud of you."

Trey waited on the sidewalk at the front door of the church. When he spotted them rounding the corner, he hurried forward, arm extended. "Hey, Hallie. Come in and see if you like this."

He directed them to the six-foot table and two chairs he'd arranged just inside the alcove leading to the sanctuary. "Pastor Dale said we could set up here. Prime real estate if we want to catch people coming in and going out."

Hallie nodded. The light-filled foyer would serve perfectly. "Looks great."

The pastor placed a hand on her shoulder and gave her a "we'll talk later" look. "I'd love to continue our conversation, if you have the time before you head back to Fort Worth."

She flashed him a smile. "I'll make time."

He glanced at his watch. "If you two have everything you need, I'll run along. I've got a scripture reference I need to check in my sermon." He winked at them before slipping through the double doors into the sanctuary.

Hallie's smile faded. He'd given her a lot to think about. Unfortunately, she knew she wasn't as magnanimous as he'd thought. What he'd mistakenly credited to her as forgiveness was nothing more than a spurt of backfired pride.

Trey was speaking. She forced her attention back to him.

"I made all the forms you and I talked about." He picked up a stack of sky-blue papers. "Here's the general information flyer. I printed a ton of them, thinking what we don't hand out this morning we can distribute around town. Not everybody will be in church, but the entire town will show up at the Grocery Giant at some point during the week. The manager said it was okay to leave them at the registers."

"You've been busy since our meeting yesterday." She took one off the top of the pile and studied it. The presentation was clean, the wording concise. Very professional. "This looks great. I'm impressed."

"Thanks."

"Thank you for clearing it with the store manager. And for making all the forms. And all the calls."

A man obviously accustomed to doing everything himself, he tipped up his broad shoulders and shrugged off her thanks. "No problem. I also typed up official-looking sign-up sheets for the committees." He pointed to a lined page. "Here's the one for the cleanup crew. I've broken it down into divisions of labor. While I was at it, I made a committee sign-up sheet for the festival as well." He placed the sheet in her hand.

She frowned at the neatly typed form. Even after their long discussion about it yesterday, she was not entirely convinced they needed a festival. To her way of thinking, a nice shout-out on the website would tie things up quite neatly.

"I thought we're keeping the festival small." She waved the paper in front of him. "This is starting to look complicated."

"We're going to want committees. Bottom line, anything we delegate, we don't have to do ourselves. You and I are both busy. Since the bulk of the festival will be food, I'd prefer someone else to be in charge." He lowered his voice. "I hate to make calls asking for food donations. My mom drags me into it for her club occasionally, and I end up stuck on the phone for hours helping decide if somebody's chocolate cake or white cake would be the right thing to bring, or did I think one or the other would be too dry?"

Hallie laughed at his comically harassed expression. "Duly noted. And if we can't get volunteers to chair the festival-food phone committee, I'll make the cookie calls."

He grinned. "Agreed."

Something in the warmth of his tone and the angle of his smile reminded her of the Trey she'd once loved. Last time she'd made that disastrous trek down memory lane, she'd almost kissed him. To break this dangerous connection, she bent her attention to the stacks of papers. "It looks like you've thought of everything, except I don't see a form for motto suggestions."

"It's here somewhere." He moved to her side, brushing close enough that she could smell his familiar soapy-clean scent. Again, she was swamped with a hundred sweet memories.

After digging around he held up a green page. "Here it is. I only provided the space for one motto per entry. But I made a pile of them so we wouldn't run out. I also printed the deadline on the bottom of the form. We'll collect submissions for a month, then pass them on to the council for voting and compiling the final ballot."

Hearing him talk about the specifics helped her drag her mind out of the misty romantic past and back into the crystal-clear, practical present. As an extra precaution because he smelled so nice, she took a step back. "That's perfect. Once we get a better idea of how long it will take to complete the renovations, we can issue updates as to when the winning motto will be announced."

He nodded. "Joe and I are meeting tomorrow morning to talk about the sidewalks and the fence around the Green. Those repairs will be the most time-consuming. He's agreed to speak to the contractors and get us a timeline."

"When we get the details, I'll post them to the website." She replaced the forms in neat piles on the table. "Thanks for giving me access to the web page. I played around with it yesterday after you left."

He grimaced. "It was pitiful, wasn't it? I knew we needed an internet presence, but I didn't take it beyond the bare bones. To be honest, I don't know the first thing about building websites."

The opportunity to showcase her extensive knowledge, and okay—brag a little—brought a smile to her face. "Go look at it when you have a chance. I changed colors and fonts to give it some pizazz and added some basic content. I'd like to see us post a calendar of town events that includes the revitalization schedule. I'll start photographing our progress and post the pictures to the website. We can use it to keep everyone informed and interest high."

The awed look on his face was priceless. "That's amazing. If we have time, maybe you can teach me how to do updates, so I can keep it current after you're gone."

Her smile widened. "I can do that."

They used the Sunday school hour to organize their table in a way to best reach the people. Hallie would man the corner closest to the door. Her responsibility would be the general information sheets and motto forms. Trey would stand beside her and monitor the committee sign-ups. They decided she could handle the big-picture discussions, and he would be best at describing the specific work to be done and the skill sets necessary to complete the tasks.

Funny, she didn't feel the stomach-gnawing dread she usually experienced with the prospect of facing the townspeople. It helped to stand behind the table, of course. She knew from her training that a podium or table between the speaker and audience gave the speaker a sense of security. But she'd be less than honest if she didn't admit Trey's presence made a big difference. With him, she felt safe.

At their lunch at Estelle's, he'd publicly expressed confidence in her competence. Then at the meeting with the chamber of commerce, he purposefully shielded her from unpleasantness and criticism. Both times he'd protected her when she was vulnerable.

Hallie tamped down the unwelcome rush of warm, fuzzy feelings. Yes, he'd been kind. Yes, she felt safe with him. But she couldn't forget he had an agenda. It was in his best interest to protect her since she was doing him a favor. He was still the enemy, the man who broke her heart.

Ten minutes before the service started, their first potential volunteers walked in the front door.

Hallie smiled. "Good morning, Mr. and Mrs. Ryder."

Mrs. Ryder wore a bright purple dress and a matching glittering purple headband in her jet-black hair. As she entered in a haze of perfume, her delighted gaze rested first on Hallie, then Trey, then back to Hallie. An unmistakably delighted matchmaking gleam shone in her eyes. "Together, *again*?" She simpered. "You two must have a lot of bank business to cover."

Hallie kept her smile firmly in place while snatching up an information sheet and motto form and handing them across the table to Mrs. Ryder. *This woman needs a hobby.* "Today it's city business. Village Green is embarking on a revitalization project, and we're getting the word out to everyone so they can join us."

Mr. Ryder elbowed his wife. "Didn't I tell you this girl was really something?"

Trey pointed to the sign-up sheet. "After you've had a chance to read over the details, we hope you'll find a place you'd like to volunteer."

"If you need more time to think about it," Hallie said, "we'll have a volunteer sign-up available on the Village Green website tomorrow as well."

Trey looked at her with raised brows, and she nodded slightly.

Mrs. Ryder frowned. "I didn't know Village Green had a website."

Trey nodded toward Hallie. "She's working on one for us. She'll be adding new details every day, so you'll want to check back often."

Mr. Ryder nudged his wife again. "Really something."

Before the organist played the opening hymn, a dozen or so people stopped by their table to ask questions and pick up forms. Hallie snapped a couple of pictures of the activity with her phone to upload to the website tonight. No time like the present to build some buzz.

When the music began, Trey stepped from behind the table and signaled Hallie to join him. "Let's grab a seat on the back pew so we can be first out the door when the service is over."

"Good idea."

Since the majority of the congregation accessed the sanctuary after Sunday school through the interior door by the altar, Hallie and Trey knew they'd have the biggest concentration of traffic when the service concluded.

She'd arranged for her mother's friends to escort her mom into the sanctuary after class. The women would sit together in their usual spot, left side, second pew from the front, freeing Hallie to deal with the information table.

The congregation was on its feet singing when Hallie and Trey entered. No one sat in the last pew on the right side, so she scooted in far enough to make room for Trey to move in beside her.

He pulled a hymnal from the rack on the back of the pew in front of them, flipped to the page listed in the bulletin and, holding the left cover in his hand, extended the right cover for her to hold.

Hallie accepted her half of the hymnal and even joined in singing, but her mind was far from the familiar words of the centuries-old song.

This must be some sort of out-of-body experience.

Never in a million years had she ever imagined she'd be standing beside Trey, in church, sharing a hymnal. No way.

Not once, in the many pleasant daydreams in which she'd visualized the humiliation and downfall of the man who'd broken her heart, had she ever pictured the two of them together in any capacity. Now they were working side by side to save the town she'd loved to hate?

Crazy.

Crazier still, she honestly hoped the revitalization worked, that the economic situation in Village Green would turn around. And not entirely because the plan had been hers. Some part of her wanted them to succeed because . . . She glanced at Trey from the corner of her eye. She didn't know why she wanted them to succeed. It was probably just more of the crazy.

CHAPTER THIRTEEN

Trey picked up his office phone on the first ring. "Mr. Gunther, Helen West is here for your nine o'clock appointment. And you've got a call on line one. Eddie Bray wants your opinion on his motto suggestion." He shook his head. So much, so soon on a Monday morning.

He indulged in an eye roll that would make a teenager proud. "Thank you, Miss Tillie. Would you ask Helen to be seated? Tell her I will be with her in just a few minutes. Tell Eddie I'm with a client. And then would you please come in here? I need to ask a favor."

"Affirmative, Mr. Gunther."

A moment later his door swung open, and Miss Tillie popped her head in.

"Come in, please. Have a seat."

Steno pad in hand, she closed the door, then hurried over to one of the leather chairs positioned in front of his desk. He busied himself with papers as she did the discreet little hop she needed to land her backside on the cushion. He'd never walked around the desk to verify it, but he was pretty certain her thick, crepe-soled shoes didn't touch the floor once she was seated.

Tillie was a mystery. She'd been with the bank for an eternity, working first for his grandfather shortly before his retirement, then his father, and now him. The wizened old woman was ancient. His dad swore she came over on the Mayflower. Trey didn't care how old she was. Tillie was smart, efficient, and most importantly, loyal. She had his back, and there was no one he'd rather have sitting at the desk outside his office.

"We have a problem."

Her wrinkled face lit with delight. Nobody enjoyed tackling a problem like Tillie. "What's up?"

"The call from Mr. Bray today was my second call this morning soliciting my advice for the motto contest."

She nodded and made a note on her pad.

"It's only going to get worse."

She nodded again and smiled. "People are surely caught up in this project."

"I'm glad. We're going to need the support and participation of everyone if we are going to make it a success. But it's going to be tough to get any bank work done with constant interruptions." He folded his hands on the desk and regarded her steadily. "I need someone to run interference."

She beamed, her eyes completely lost in the myriad crinkles. "I make an excellent screen, sir."

He grinned. "I'm counting on it. When those calls come in, I want you to tell them I'm not able to consult on mottos. Tell them that as a potential judge for the contest, there is a conflict of interest. I can't see anyone crying foul over it, but I think we'd be wise to prevent problems from developing."

"I agree." Tillie frowned. "I guess that means you don't want to hear the slogan I came up with." She smiled. "I'm telling you, it's a doozy."

He chewed the insides of his mouth to keep from laughing. "I'm tempted, but I think I'd better not. We wouldn't want to give anyone reason to accuse us of collusion."

"Good point. Although I know you're going to love it when you hear it."

He chewed harder. "Are we good? If so, would you send Helen in?"

She glanced at the line or two of notes she'd written on her tablet while he spoke. "Got it. Our mission is strict neutrality. You are unable to consult on mottos because of possible conflict of interest." She scooted forward on the chair and hopped to the floor. "I'll get the word out. You can count on me."

He smiled while she headed to the door. "I do, Miss Tillie. I really do."

Seconds later Tillie ushered Helen into the office. "Would you care for coffee or tea, Mrs. West?"

"Oh, no thank you. I'm fine."

Trey came around his desk to take Helen's hand in greeting. "Good morning. Please forgive me for making you wait. Things are a little crazy around here after the announcement of the revitalization project."

"I don't mind." She glanced at him briefly before self-consciously dropping her gaze to the carpet. "It's exciting to think of Village Green coming alive again."

He directed her to one of the chairs in front of his desk and took the seat beside her. "It is exciting. And I think we can use it to our advantage to sell your farm."

Her gaze flew to his. "How so?"

"Property in a depressed area sells cheaply, frequently at a loss. But a home and farm in an up-and-coming location should fetch top dollar."

Her expression was hopeful. "Do you really think so? That would be amazing. An answer to prayer."

So many possibilities were suddenly on the table because of the planned improvements. New jobs, more business opportunities.

His prayer for a plan to address the town's troubles had certainly been answered. "Seems like there is a lot of answered prayer going around right now."

He scooped her file from the corner of his desk. "I've got all the numbers here." He opened the folder and propped it between them. "Here's the breakdown of the price you and Elmer paid for the farm, the equity you've accrued, and the balance owed. We'll want these figures to determine the asking price for the property."

He flipped to the page beneath it. "In addition, I've researched comps for the most recent land sales in our county and the adjoining ones. These will tell us what others have received for their land and help us fine-tune the price we want to set for our listing."

After studying the information, she folded her hands in her lap and sighed deeply. "There's a lot to selling a farm, isn't there?"

"Second thoughts?"

"No, I definitely want to sell. I know I need to sell, but . . ."

He studied her face for a moment, saw the worry lines, and closed the folder. "Let's ease back a little, shall we? I know you want to sell, but there is no reason we need to finalize anything today. Why don't you take this information home and look it over? We can meet to talk about it next Monday if that works for you. I'll come out to your place and save you the trip into town if that would be helpful."

"Thank you, but I'm making an effort to get out more, so I'll meet you here at the bank."

Trey could tell by the determination in her voice, it truly was an effort. "Sure, whatever works for you."

"I hardly left the house when things with Elmer got so bad, then when he died . . ." She lapsed into silence. "I just didn't want to be with anyone."

He nodded. "Grief can be like that."

Helen studied her hands. "People have been so kind to me, you and others, by coming out to visit and telephoning to check on me. Part of me could go on like that forever, hidden away on the farm with my memories."

She shifted slightly, squared her shoulders, and met Trey's gaze. "The other day I looked at myself in the mirror and thought Elmer would be ashamed of me. We knew he was dying, of course, so we had plenty of time to talk about the future . . ." She swallowed hard before continuing. "Without him."

Blinking back tears, Helen continued, "He said he'd come back and haunt me if I holed up in the house like a recluse." Her voice wasn't quite steady. "So here I am."

Her courage in the face of so much loss was humbling. Trey prayed the revitalization worked, if only for her sake, so she had an opportunity to live and thrive. "You're a very brave woman, Mrs. West, and I believe your husband would be proud. I hope you'll let me help you in any way I can."

Helen nodded. "Thank you. Right now, you can help me by making me come into town for our appointments."

He smiled. "I can do that. Any plans for this morning when you leave here?"

"I thought about running by to see Leah Nichols. I haven't talked to her since her stroke. I should call first to be sure it's a good time." Mrs. West frowned. "I've neglected my friends so badly over the past year. It's awkward to call them."

"Then let me make the call for you. I need to ask Hallie a question about the revitalization project anyway. While we're on the phone, I'll just ask if they are up for a visit."

Helen sighed. "If it's not too much trouble, that would be wonderful. But be sure it's a good time—I don't want to impose."

CHAPTER FOURTEEN

Hallie's mother shuffled from the room in a bad-tempered huff. She'd become quite adept at communicating her displeasure with the four plastic-tipped prongs at the end of her cane. Thump. Thump. Thump.

The measure of Hallie's disgrace was in direct proportion to the crash of the cane on the floor. Based on the current reverberations, she was in deep disfavor.

Her cell phone rang. Her spirits lifted immediately and certainly not because it was Trey's name that appeared on the screen. "Hello?"

"Did I catch you at a good time?"

Since when did the sound of his voice do weird things to her nerve endings? "I guess that depends on who you're talking to. Me? I'm good. Mom? Not so much."

"Uh-oh."

She turned, facing her back to the door, and lowered her voice. "Yeah. We just had an epic showdown. I told her we had appointments to visit several assisted living centers today, and she went ballistic."

He sighed. "I'm really sorry. I thought she understood that's her next step."

"It's not a matter of understanding so much as agreement. She doesn't think she should have to move. She feels I should drop everything, move in, and take care of her full-time."

"Does that mean she's given up on your sister?"

She plopped down at the kitchen table and propped her chin in her hands. "Apparently. It seems Janice's place is at her husband's side, fulfilling her heaven-ordained role of wife to an important football coach. I, on the other hand, have no such calling or commitments and can easily set aside my paltry existence to serve her as any grateful daughter would want to do."

"Ouch."

"No kidding." Hallie sighed. "Sorry. I didn't mean to unload on you. I'm just frustrated. I've got to make those appointments, and I wanted her to come with me to choose her new home. Plus, I could keep an eye on her. She won't fall if I'm there to catch her." Another sigh. "Everything I've read says you should look at these places in pairs. The theory being the second set of eyes might catch what the first set misses. If I go alone, I may overlook something important."

"Hey, I may have a solution for you. Hold on a sec while I ask." He was back on the phone moments later. "Helen West is here at the bank with me. She was planning to drop by and visit your mother this morning if it was convenient. I just told her about your appointments, and she says she'd love to stay with your mom while you're gone."

"Really? That would be amazing." Her joy at finding an answer to her problems was short-lived. "But I could be gone for three hours. I can't ask her to stay that long."

She heard him convey the information.

"Helen says no problem. She and your mom have a lot to catch up on."

"Wow. Thank you, Trey. I don't know if you could hear it through the phone, but a ton of pressure just fell from my shoulders."

He chuckled. "I'm glad. I probably owe it to you after roping you into the revitalization, which is the original reason why I called you. I talked with Joe, and he gave me some projected time frames. I wanted to run them by you." He paused. "I have an idea. Why don't I go with you to the appointments this morning? On the drive between facilities, we can talk about project details."

The surge of pleasure she felt at his suggestion was simply a product of her vast relief. After all, if Trey came with her, she'd have another pair of eyes to evaluate the assisted living centers. "Can you do that? I could use the backup."

"Be glad to. What time are the appointments?"

"They are both in Corsicana. One is at eleven. The other is at noon. According to Google Maps, the buildings are within four miles of each other."

"Perfect. Helen and I can be at your place in fifteen minutes or so."

"That's great. We'll see you then."

Hallie disconnected the call and headed to her closet. She needed an outfit that said take this woman seriously, and now that Trey was coming, it would be a plus if it happened to make her look amazing. She dressed in a pink silk blouse and black slacks with a pair of black heels, a tad lower than her Superwoman shoes. Her reflection in the narrow mirror on the back of her bedroom door said two thumbs up.

She'd just brewed a fresh pot of iced tea when she heard the knock at the front door. She hurried out of the kitchen and down the hall to greet Trey and Mrs. West.

"Welcome." She waved them inside and pulled Mrs. West into a hug. "It's wonderful to see you. I was so sorry to hear about Mr.

West. He was a wonderful man. I'll always remember him with a little spark of mischief in his eyes."

Helen smiled. "Thank you. He was a first-class cutup, that's for certain. And thank you again for the flowers you sent. The arrangement was beautiful. It was sweet of you to remember us."

"Hello, Helen," Hallie's mother called from her perch on the chair. "I'm so glad you're here. Come sit with me. I want to hear all about you."

Helen crossed the room and bent to hug her friend. "It feels like it's been ages. I've missed you, Leah."

Helen settled into the chair near Hallie's mom and the two instantly fell into conversation.

Watching them together, Hallie felt the residual tension in her shoulders ease. Her mom would be in good hands. "May I get you ladies a glass of tea before Trey and I go?"

Hallie's mother gave a short shake of her head, obviously still angry.

Helen smiled. "No, thank you. I'm fine right now. If we get thirsty later, I can fix us each a glass, if that's okay with you?"

Hallie nodded. *Okay? Anyone willing to babysit my mother has my blessing to do whatever she pleases.* "Absolutely. And if you get hungry while we're gone, there are all sorts of sandwich fixings in the refrigerator. Please help yourself to anything you find."

"Thank you," said Helen.

"I anticipate we'll be gone about two and a half hours. We'll hurry, but between travel time and the actual appointments, I don't think we'll be back before two o'clock."

"That's fine," Helen reassured her with a breezy wave. "As I told Trey, Leah and I have a lot to catch up on."

Hallie walked out the door with a sense of freedom she hadn't known since before her mother's stroke. The warm sun on her face underscored her lightheartedness.

She turned to Trey. "Thank you."

He smiled. "For what?"

"Are you kidding? Your bringing Helen here this morning saved the day. Possibly my life. I feel like a kid skipping school."

He grinned. "I'm glad. And you're welcome."

At the foot of the stairs, he stopped and pointed to his truck. "Why don't I drive? I have the general idea where we're going, and you can navigate us in as we get closer."

"Okay, good idea. Thanks."

He opened the passenger door, waited until she'd slid in and fastened her seat belt, then closed the door behind her. Hallie sat back, strangely aware of the intimacy of riding in Trey's truck. They'd sat this close at Estelle's, and it never bothered her. Probably because a table separated them. The same thing was true when he'd eaten at her mother's house or met her at his office. Each time a piece of furniture acted as a buffer between them. Even sitting side by side in the pew on Sunday when they'd been mere inches apart didn't feel as private as it did right now, probably because they shared the sanctuary with a hundred others.

Trey rounded the truck and climbed in behind the wheel. If he felt unsettled being confined in the cab of a truck with her, it didn't show.

He fired up the engine, then picked up the file lying on the seat and handed it to her. "Those are the numbers Joe got this morning from the contractors about the sidewalks. He faxed them to me after his meeting. Even though you're not directly involved with the construction phase, I wanted you to look them over, especially the estimated start and completion dates. I think this piece of the project, being the biggest, will ultimately determine how quickly we can wrap things up."

"I agree." Hallie opened the folder and scanned down the page to the numbers typed at the bottom. "Omigosh!" She whipped her head around to face him. "I had no idea replacing a few sidewalks would be so expensive. How in the world will you pay for this?"

"We've had several private donors come forward and offer to cover the costs." The closed look on his face told her Trey was one of those donors. And that he wouldn't be making the information public.

"Doesn't the city have *any* money for this project?"

Eyes on the road, he shrugged. "We've got a small miscellaneous fund we can tap, but if we don't want to borrow money, we'll have to rely on donations for the big stuff."

"Oh." She frowned. She should have known anything this size would have to be privately funded. He'd told her from the beginning that Village Green was broke.

For some reason, the knowledge that people were staking their own money on her suggestion upped her personal emotional ante. Suddenly it went from theory to reality. The project had to work. She'd be sick if anyone wasted their hard-earned cash because of her.

She read the figures one more time before closing the folder. "Yikes."

"Scary, huh?"

"Terrifying." She replaced the file on the seat between them. "After seeing those numbers, I'm not sure I'll be able to sleep tonight."

He gave her one of the reassuring smiles that made him a successful banker. "Relax. Everything worthwhile involves some risk. Your plan is sound. This is a gamble we're willing to take."

Hallie swallowed hard at his word choice. Gamble? Double yikes.

She was quiet as Trey steered them through town and out onto the highway heading south to Corsicana.

"Tell me the plan for the appointments today." He glanced in her direction. "What do we want to see happen?"

She turned from the window to look at him. "I want to get a feel for the places, to see if they would be a good fit for my mother. Of course, in a perfect world, she'd be going with me since the decision affects her directly, but in her current mood maybe it's best she stayed behind."

Hallie pressed her lips together. "I've looked at the ratings online, and both of the places we'll be seeing have good reviews. But I want to see these places in person. If we find something we like, I need to get actual prices so we'll know exactly what it will cost per month for Mom to live there. I also want to find out about specific services—will they drive her to doctors' appointments, do they offer physical therapy on-site—those sorts of things."

"It sounds like you've done your homework."

"I have." She sighed and watched the landscape speed by. "This is a big deal. Despite what my mother says, I'm not trying to put her away. I want to find a good, safe environment for her to live in."

She turned to Trey. "This may not even be a forever thing. The doctor says with time and exercise, she could regain full use of her arm and leg. If she experiences that level of recovery, it's possible she could live independently again."

"You know, you'd be making your life a whole lot easier if you moved her to an assisted living center in Fort Worth."

She nodded. "Trust me, I've thought of that. But in Fort Worth she'd be so far from her friends. I'd hate for her to be lonely."

He smiled. "I've said it before. You're a good daughter."

Hallie keyed the first address into the map app on her phone when they passed the city limit sign. Five minutes and a few turns later, they pulled into the parking lot of Nurture Assisted Living Center.

Trey switched off the ignition. "Looks nice on the outside."

Hallie nodded. The one-story, red brick building spread across the wide grassy lot like a comfortably rambling ranch style house. "High marks for curb appeal. Let's see what we think of the inside."

She pulled a notecard from her handbag to refresh her memory. "Our appointment is with a Ms. Anthony at eleven."

Trey glanced at his watch. "We're right on time. Let's go."

They met up in front of the truck and walked side by side to the arched entrance. Hallie paused, laid a hand on his forearm, and lifted her eyes to his. "I really appreciate this. More than I can say."

When she returned home two weeks ago, his presence had felt like a splinter, an uncomfortable annoyance to be rid of. Just seeing him was a painful reminder of rejection and hurts too deep for words. But at the chamber meeting and yesterday at church, she'd been glad to have him nearby. She'd never be foolish enough to trust him with her heart, but honestly, she'd enjoyed his company. He was fun. He'd made her feel safe. They'd made a good team. Today while facing important decisions, she felt stronger, more in control because he stood with her.

Maybe they could be friends. The unexpected thought rocked her. Not the "let's hang out" variety, of course, they had too much history for that, but the kind of friend who liked you and wanted the best for you. The kind of friends who went their separate ways, but when their paths crossed down the line, they could meet with a smile.

She was still processing the mind-boggling discovery when they arrived at the door. A middle-aged woman dressed in a navy business suit met them just inside. "Hallie Nichols?"

Hallie stepped forward and extended her hand. "Yes. I'm Hallie. And this is my, uh friend, Trey Gunther. You must be Ms. Anthony."

"I am. Welcome." After shaking hands, she looked beyond Hallie and Trey. "I don't see your mother. Is she—?"

"She wasn't feeling up to a visit this morning."

Ms. Anthony nodded. "No problem. She's welcome to come another time, or she can rely on you to do the legwork. If you two are ready, we can start with a tour of the building. Then we'll go back to my office to answer any questions you may have."

The tour lasted about half an hour and encompassed all the public spaces and examples of the different types of apartments available to tenants. Ms. Anthony appeared to be well-known and liked by the residents, and the three of them stopped frequently for a chat with people using walkers or canes or speeding around on scooters.

They paused outside the television room, and Hallie glanced around. "Everything looks nice and tidy and smells so fresh."

Ms. Anthony beamed. "Thank you. We're really proud of our facility. You can imagine that with fifty people living under the same roof, it can be challenging, but we have a full-time cleaning and maintenance staff committed to the upkeep."

Trey pointed to the far wall. "I like all the windows."

She smiled. "One of the comments I hear most often is that Nurture is so homey. I attribute a good part of that to our abundant natural light."

The tour wound up in Ms. Anthony's office in the administrative suite. "Do you have any questions?"

Hallie laughed and pulled a sheet of paper from her purse. "Dozens."

Ms. Anthony addressed the available services first. When they'd covered the questions, she brought out the price list, and they reviewed costs based on what Hallie perceived her mother would want. Hallie was grateful the woman was a low-key saleswoman and never applied pressure.

"If this is the place we choose for my mother, when could she move in?"

Ms. Anthony knew the answer without referring to her notes. "We have an apartment in the east wing that will be available in two weeks. The current resident will be moving to a skilled nursing facility."

Trey had been pretty quiet during their meeting. "If she decides she wants it, how soon would Hallie need to reserve the apartment in the east wing?"

Ms. Anthony folded her hands on the desk. "Honestly, as soon as possible. When you make your decision, I will ask you to give us a deposit which is the equivalent of the first month's rent. That deposit will hold the space for you. If someone else puts in a deposit before you, the apartment is theirs, and you would have to wait until the next availability."

Hallie grimaced. "Are there others looking?"

The saleswoman gave her a sympathetic smile and nodded. "Ours is a very popular facility."

A knot of anxiety lodged in Hallie's chest. The next appointment did nothing to remove it. Assisted living space was limited, and the clock was ticking.

Trey pulled out of the parking lot of the second facility into the light, local traffic. "So, what are your thoughts?"

She sighed. "Where to begin?"

Eyes trained on the road, he nodded. "Yeah, I know what you mean. It's been an information overload kind of morning. But I was encouraged by what we saw. Both facilities seemed clean, the staff members were nice, and the residents looked happy and engaged."

"I agree. The food was even okay." She looked at him and laughed. "I wish you could have seen your expression when I accepted the saleswoman's invitation to eat lunch in the dining room. I don't think horrified is too strong a word to describe it."

He glanced over at her and joined in her laughter. "No kidding. I couldn't believe you actually said yes. I swear I saw my life flash before my eyes. I had visions of plastic trays piled with lumps of unidentifiable goo. I was pleasantly surprised—make that relieved—when the food arrived in easily recognizable form, served on china plates. And with a little salt and pepper."

She snorted a laugh. "A lot of salt and pepper, you mean. I couldn't see the surface of your chicken because of the layer of salt you dumped on it. And don't get me started on the ketchup."

He grinned. "Okay, I admit it was a lot of salt and pepper. And ketchup. Anyway, the food was okay. And the cake was delicious. I did think the servings could be larger."

Obviously, since he'd eaten his piece and half of hers. "Which place did you like better?"

He pressed his lips together for a moment. "I liked them both. I think either place would be comfortable and safe for your mom. If I had to choose, I think I preferred the first place. Both facilities were nice, but Nurture just seemed a notch above."

Hallie nodded. "That would be my first choice too. It totally freaked me out when she said I needed to put in my deposit right away. I thought I'd have more time to mull it over." She pushed a hand through her hair. "This is moving much faster than I anticipated."

"Yeah, I was surprised by the short supply of available apartments."

She caught her lower lip in her teeth. "Me too. I guess this is one of those things you don't give much thought to until you're neck deep in it. After talking with the salespeople this morning, I feel the water quickly rising above my ears."

"I'm sorry. It's a lot to decide. Especially when your mother isn't cooperating." He glanced over. "Have you spoken to Janice? Has she weighed in on what she thinks is the best solution for your mom?"

Hallie shrugged. "She says she'll back whatever decision I make. They are in spring training right now, so she's busy with all that . . ."

They lapsed into a comfortable silence as the truck sped down the highway toward home. In spite of the ball of anxiety wedged behind her ribcage, it had been a fun day. Even difficult tasks were easier with a friend.

She and Trey. Friends.

She hadn't seen it coming, but she had to admit it had been nice to have a friend today, to share her burdens and help her with major decisions.

As nice as it was, some part of her was uneasy with their new status. Friendship meant vulnerability, and vulnerability with Trey was bad. Ten years ago, she'd trusted him with her heart, and he'd crushed it. She needed to keep her guard up. Casual friendship was fine, but anything beyond it was a sure setup for pain.

CHAPTER FIFTEEN

O ver the next few days Hallie did a lot of thinking about friendship and forgiveness. Interspersed between handling the
demands of her company—thank heaven for a capable assistant—
fielding calls about the revitalization project and dealing with her
mother's needs and moods, her thoughts returned often to Pastor
Dale's words, "I'm proud of you for extending forgiveness."

The problem with the whole forgiveness thing the pastor com-
mended her for was that she knew for a fact she'd never actually
given it. Not to the town, not to her mother or sister, not even to
Trey. She'd never once made the conscious decision to release the
wounds of the past and the people who inflicted them so she could
walk forward unencumbered.

Truthfully, she'd clung to the hurts, using them to focus her
energy and propel her life to success.

That didn't sound like a recipe for healthy living.

She knew unforgiveness ripened into bitterness. She'd seen
the inescapable pattern played out in other people's lives dozens of
times. Had it happened to her? Was she bitter?

She checked her reflection in the bathroom mirror, turning her
face from side to side beneath the bright fluorescent bulbs, looking for the telltale signs. Bitterness showed up in all kinds of places.
A brittle gleam in the eyes, uncompromising lines bracketing the

mouth, a harsh tone of voice. Left to run its course, bitterness permeated the body and spirit, tainting every aspect of life.

Was that where she was headed?

She examined her life objectively—her words, attitudes, and actions. It didn't take a genius to see she already exhibited signs of hardening.

At one time, she'd convinced herself hardening was good, a natural process in which a protective layer of scar tissue formed to prevent reinjury. Suddenly, she saw it for what it was—self-destructiveness that would ultimately lead to isolation.

She didn't want the ugly taint staining her life. But to release the bitterness meant she'd have to forgive. And that was the sticking point. Because if she forgave those people, she was letting them off the hook. It was as if she were saying what they did was okay. But it wasn't okay. Their words and actions were wrong, and she couldn't pretend they didn't happen. She had the scars to prove it.

Day after day her thoughts traveled the same worn path. The only escape from bitterness was forgiveness. Time after time she came up hard against the same wall. If forgiveness meant excusing those who'd hurt her, she couldn't do it.

After a particularly difficult day with her mother, Hallie fell into bed with a heavy heart. Her mother had been balky and unreasonable. And Hallie had responded with impatience and anger.

Her mother had an excuse. The stroke affected her physically and emotionally, and she was making the difficult uphill climb toward coming to terms with her radically altered life.

Hallie had no excuse. She was healthy and strong, but her actions were every bit as childish as her mother's. She'd let her mother's negativity and lopsided comparisons with her sister wear her down until they'd fallen into a routine of snapped answers and sulky silences.

It was up to Hallie to make the change.

Too agitated to sleep, she rolled over on her side to pray. *"Dear Lord, I need Your help. You see the mess here, Mom and I squabbling like two-year-olds. I hate it—I'm truly ashamed of myself, but I don't know how to change—"*

Deep conviction hit her like a sudden wave, and she stopped in mid-sentence. *"Okay, yes, I do know how to change it. Forgiveness. That's what You've been showing me all along, isn't it? The only way I'll be able to improve my relationship with my mother is to forgive her. But I can't. It's impossible."*

No sooner had the word escaped her lips, than a scripture came to mind with such crystal clarity she wasn't sure it hadn't been audible. "With God all things are possible." It was as if she and the Almighty were face-to-face, and He was personally answering her objections.

Unnerved, she bolted upright in bed. She waited a moment in the darkness, tilting her head from side to side. Nothing.

"Okay," she prompted. *"I'm listening. Does that mean You'll help me forgive her? Because barring a supernatural move, I don't see it happening."*

"I can do all things through him who strengthens me."

There it was again. The words flashed into her mind so rapidly, with such finality, it felt like a spoken reply. She sat, listening in the dark, waiting to see if there was more. Or if her bedspread suddenly burst into flames without being consumed.

No sound. No fire.

"Okay, it's settled then. I'm going to forgive my mom with the strength You give me." She paused to see if there was a reply. Silence. *"Thank You. I'm . . . uh, glad we had this talk."*

A little spooked, Hallie hunkered down under the covers and squeezed her eyes shut. Still wide awake ten minutes later, she realized the holy interaction was not yet complete.

She opened her eyes and sighed in resignation. *"We're not done yet, are we? No sleep until I put it all on the line."* She scooted into a seated position. *"Okay. I'll do it. Really. If You'll help me, I'll forgive them all. Everyone. I mean it. I'll do my part if You'll do Yours."* Honesty had her adding, *"This is going to be really tough. I'm going to need a lot of help. And I'm going to need You to show me what my part is."*

"Trust in the LORD with all your heart, and do not lean on your own understanding. In all your ways acknowledge him, and he will make straight your paths."

She lay back against the pillow, pulling up the covers again. *"I don't know how You're going to do it. But then, I don't have to. Because You're God and I'm not."* She yawned. *"Goodnight. And thank You."*

"Thank you so much for coming, Mrs. West." Hallie stepped aside for her to enter.

She frowned. "Now Hallie, I told you to call me Helen," she scolded in her gentle voice. "And you don't have to keep thanking me as though I'm doing you a big favor. I like being here."

"But Mrs. West, I mean, Helen, you are doing me a huge favor. Mom has completely refused to do her exercises with me. And the doctor warned us that her physical therapy twice a week isn't enough. I've already seen so much improvement just since you two started working on them together."

Helen lifted a hand to stop her. "The blessing has been entirely mine. I enjoy spending time with your mother. I've needed something to do. Since Elmer died, I've been drifting through the days. Seeing Leah and working with her has given me purpose. I should really be thanking you. Now, shouldn't you be running along? I think you said something about an eleven o'clock appointment."

Hallie pulled out her phone and checked the time. "You're right. I'd better get going. I should be back at one. One thirty at the latest."

Helen gave her a motherly pat. "We'll be fine. Take your time."

Hallie grabbed her tote, called out a goodbye to her mother, and trotted down the front stairs to her car. She'd driven to the bank so many times over the last couple of days, she felt she could do it blindfolded. Village Green Bank and Trust had become home base for the revitalization project. Mr. Gunther had graciously given them use of the large conference room to house forms and supplies, sparing Hallie from setting up shop in her mother's tiny living room.

She parked in a spot in front of the bank, hiked her tote onto her shoulder, and hurried inside.

"Good morning, Mr. Swinton." She gave him a cheery wave as she breezed through the lobby.

Miss Tillie looked up when Hallie approached her desk. "Are you and Trey meeting in the war room this morning? I've already unlocked it and turned on your computer." She picked up the phone. "I'll tell him you're here. Can I bring you a cup of coffee?"

Hallie shook her head. "No thanks for the coffee. And I'm early, so please don't interrupt Trey if he's busy. I have plenty to keep me occupied."

Miss Tillie nodded. "We've had a lot more motto submissions dropped off here. I put them in a stack on the table with a note. You'll see them. Mine is the one on top."

Hallie paused. "I thought you'd already submitted one."

"I had. But then, in the middle of the night, another one popped in my head." She snapped gnarled fingers. "I think it's better than the first. You're going to love it."

Hallie grinned. "I'm sure I will."

She continued down the hall to the conference room and switched on the overhead lights. She stopped just inside the door, struck by the difference a couple of weeks made. The first time she appeared here, it was to white-knuckle her presentation in front of a semi-hostile audience. Her best recollection of that morning was nerves and nausea. The spacious room had felt claustrophobic, and she'd been counting the minutes until she could escape.

Today, the room felt like her personal, oversized office. She scanned the stacks of paper lined up along the mahogany table. Miss Tillie was right. They'd amassed a sizable pile of entries. She scooped them up on her way to the computer in the corner.

Hallie slipped her bag off her shoulder and set it on the floor beside the desk. She logged in with the password Trey had assigned her and got down to work. Over the last week, she'd developed a rhythm. First, she checked the city website. If she'd snapped any usable pictures the day before, she'd upload them to the revitalization page. Then she'd look to see if there was any activity on the volunteer sign-up page. She'd transfer that information to the duplicate chart she kept in the war room. If there were any comments or questions, she'd address them. When the website was updated, she'd go to the file she'd created for storing motto submissions.

She and Trey had decided the best, fairest way to judge the entries was to separate the name of the person who'd submitted it from the motto itself. The nominating committee would be presented with an anonymous list of submissions and select their top ten without the influence of favoritism. The system wasn't perfect, of course. People were free to tell their mottos to others, but knowing they couldn't control every variable, it seemed the best, most expedient approach.

Hallie had volunteered to type the entries into the file. The rationale being that as the only nonresident on the committee, she was the most unbiased. This morning after a quick perusal of the website, she opened the file and began entering the newest submissions.

"You're here so often, I'm beginning to think we should add you to the payroll."

Trey's whispered remark, delivered two inches from her right ear, startled her. She squeaked and clapped a hand over her racing heart. "I didn't hear you come in." She turned to send him a saucy grin. "And no, I believe we've already discussed it and concluded you can't afford me."

He sighed. "True. If you were too expensive before, by now we've run up a tab we could never pay." His expression grew serious. "I hope you know how grateful I am. The time and energy you've put in—you've been amazing."

She shrugged it off. "It's been fun. I've enjoyed it."

It was fun, and she had enjoyed it. She loved public relations. It was immensely satisfying to polish and fine-tune a raw product, and when it showed to its full potential to market it. The challenge of applying the basic PR principles to the city had already expanded her understanding of promoting a client and opened a new world of possibilities for future business opportunities.

It had come as a surprise that she enjoyed working for Village Green. She found herself hurrying through her company-related responsibilities so she could focus on the revitalization. She'd never dreamed working side by side with Trey to save his dying town would fill her with such a heady rush of pleasure and energy.

He parked a hip on the corner of the conference table. "Tell you what. In lieu of a salary, let me take you to lunch. I'm starving, and we can talk project over Estelle's fried chicken."

She cocked her brow. "With dessert?"

"You drive a hard bargain." He laughed. "Of course you can have dessert. We can negotiate on the way as to whether you get your own or have to share mine."

She nodded. "It's a deal. Let me enter these last two mottos, then we can go."

Instead of moving away, Trey stayed beside her. The weight of his gaze made her fingers clumsy. She gave him a pointed look. "Don't you have something to do?"

He flashed a grin. "Nope." He folded his arms across his chest. "I'm happy right here."

She did her best to ignore him while she finished typing and logged out. "Let's eat."

"You looked pretty engrossed in whatever you were doing." He glanced at the stack of papers she had been working on. "The mottos are that good, huh?"

She nodded. "There are a few cute ones."

"Are you going to submit one?"

Hallie's laugh was self-conscious. She told herself she was okay with them being friends, but when he looked at her like he was just now, giving her the full attention of his golden laser focus, well, it made her feel jittery. Like one too many glasses of iced tea. She dropped her gaze to the papers. "I don't know. I hadn't planned on it. I thought it might be problematic since I'm cochairing the project."

"I don't see why it would. We're not motto judges, so nobody can complain about bias. And your entry will be anonymous. The judges won't know who submitted what. You should do it."

"Are you?"

"I would if I could think of one. So far, I've got nothing. What would your motto be?"

"The place where you belong." She tipped up her shoulders in a dismissive shrug. "I thought it would look nice painted on the sign coming into town.

"I like it. Positive and assertive." When she lifted her eyes to his, he smiled and added, "Just like you."

Positive and assertive.

He wouldn't have used those words to describe the Hallie he knew in high school. He wouldn't even have used those words to describe the Hallie who blew into town a month ago. High school Hallie was sweet and shy. Month-ago Hallie had learned to speak up for herself and had gained a world of self-confidence, but she was prickly and spoiling for a fight. The best description for month-ago Hallie was angry with attitude. The woman at his side today, Hallie 3.0, was the best version of Hallie.

She was confident without being overbearing. She wasn't afraid to speak her mind, but she paid others the courtesy of hearing them out. The simmering anger and resentment she'd carried so close to the surface when she first arrived in town seemed to have disappeared. In its place, he saw a determination to look for the positive.

He shut off the lights in the conference room and pulled the door closed behind them as they stepped into the hall. "Is Helen with your mother this morning?"

Hallie nodded. "She's been there nearly every day for at least an hour so they can do exercises. Can you believe my mom *likes* to do exercises with Helen? I actually heard them giggling. Like they are having fun."

"I didn't realize they were such good friends." He waved to Miss Tillie when they walked past her desk.

"Me either. Helen told me Mom gives her purpose. Both times I've had to go to Fort Worth, Helen has spent the day with her. That's going beyond the bounds of friendship." She stopped just before they exited the relative privacy of the executive wing and looked up at him. "Do you think I should pay her for her time? She's certainly earned it, but I would hate to offend her."

He frowned. "I'm afraid it might."

"I'm not sure what her financial situation is like since her husband has passed away, but I imagine she could use the money."

Trey knew for a fact Helen would need to find employment but wouldn't divulge her personal business. "Maybe you two could sit down and discuss it. Although, I'm guessing you won't need her to babysit much longer. What have you decided to do about the assisted living center?"

They continued down the hall and through the lobby. "Nothing yet. I took your suggestion and invited Mom and Helen to take the tour of Nurture together, but my mom flat refuses. She won't even look at the place. It's crazy, but I think she's holding out to force me to stay here and take care of her."

The same thing had occurred to him. Mrs. Nichols had dug her heels in, determined not to yield to the inevitable move. She wanted her daughter to remain. Interestingly enough, he was beginning to feel the same way. Life was just better with Hallie here.

From the moment she'd stormed into his office, demanding he keep his Gunther nose out of her family's business, things had taken a distinct upturn—much of which was directly related to the revitalization, of course. Once a lone man, searching fruitlessly for solutions, he now had a plan and a partner to labor beside him. Whether or not they were successful, it had been great to share the burden with Hallie.

More than that, she made him feel more alive than he had in years. Which sounded weird, but it was true. Case in point. This morning, instead of rolling over to grab a few more minutes of sleep when the alarm went off, he was out of bed in a flash, excited about the day's possibilities.

Correction. Excited to see Hallie.

He glanced down at her and held open the door for her to exit the building. If the anger he'd sensed in her was gone, did that mean she'd changed her thinking about Village Green? Would she ever consider relocating here?

Only one way to find out.

He stepped from the sidewalk and onto the street beside her. "And that's out of the question, right? About you moving back here, I mean." The supremely casual remark was half statement, half question. All fishing. He watched her carefully and waited for her reply.

The sunlight highlighted the variations in shade of her dark waves when she shook her head. "It would never work. My relationship with my mom hasn't improved since I got here. We'd murder each other in a matter of weeks. Besides, my company is in Fort Worth."

This was progress. It took her a moment to answer him just now, and when she did finally speak, her words were thoughtful, an improvement over the instant explosion of vitriol for the same question a month ago. He was an idiot to be cheered by the moderation of her response. But he couldn't help it.

Maybe she was coming around.

They crossed the street to the Green. Since the project began, the sidewalks had been cordoned off with barricades and miles of police tape. A separate walkway for pedestrians had been created alongside the original, like a ring around Saturn, delineated by orange safety cones and more tape.

The construction crew that Joe hired out of Fort Worth was replacing the crumbling hundred-year-old concrete in sections, leaving openings for public access to the Green. So far, the north and east sides of the sidewalk were complete, though still blocked off, and the crew was currently tackling the south end of the park. The ear-splitting staccato of the jackhammers had become a familiar sound to the town.

Hallie tented a hand over her eyes to study the Green. "It's moving right along."

"With the weather cooperating, they've been able to stay on schedule." He raised the folder he carried in his right hand. "I've got the latest projections with me. I think you and I can safely set the festival date."

"Hard to believe, isn't it? It's really happening." She glanced down. "The new sidewalk looks amazing. I'm still not sure I understand how they aged the concrete, but it really does look old."

"Joe explained it to me, something about color pigment embedded in the mixture. I admit, I was skeptical when they proposed it, but it's perfect for the historical look we're going for."

She stopped and pointed. "Speaking of history, what are they doing to the gazebo?" Her pretty mouth turned down. "I thought it had been slated for demolition."

"Last minute reprieve. Mary Jo Piermont apparently had a soft spot for it and told Mayor Sellers she'd pay to have it refurbished. Going back to your model about whether it supports the look and feel we're going for—rich history and family friendly. We decided to keep it. In fact, Mayor Sellers wants to use it as the focal point for the festival. We'll wire it for sound and lights and use it as our stage. It'll make a great place to announce the winning motto."

"I guess so."

Hallie didn't sound convinced, and he was hard-pressed to understand how an old wooden structure engendered such strong feelings. According to the mayor, Mary Jo Piermont came to him in tears, pleading with him to save the gazebo. Hallie, on the other hand, had been nearly as vehement in her determination to remove the "blight" from the Green.

The way he saw it, if they could rebuild it strong and functional on Ms. Piermont's dime, it would make a nice architectural feature on the Green. A landmark for tourists to see.

They passed through an opening in the tape, crossed the street, and stepped up onto the sidewalk about two blocks from Estelle's. Because of time and financial constraints, the walkways in front of the shops were deemed good enough to wait for a phase two of the revitalization. Blue handbills for the project were stapled at regular intervals on the rough plywood covering the old storefronts.

Hallie looked up and sighed. "I wish I knew what we could do with these empty shops. Miles of decaying boards don't exactly say welcome to our cozy town."

Trey lifted a brow. Our town? That sounded promising.

"I agree. And I don't think the new plywood we plan to replace the old boards with will be any less of an eyesore." He thought for a moment, then grinned. "I suppose we could paint welcome on them in really big letters."

"That's it!"

He loved it when her face lit up like that. "Really? I was kidding—"

"I know, but it's actually a great idea." Her pace increased with her excitement. "We'll paint them. Not with the word welcome, but with some kind of mural. Something Texas-y."

He hated to kill her enthusiasm, but finances figured largely in his thoughts right now. "And do you happen to have a muralist on speed dial? One who would offer his or her services gratis? We can spring for the paint, but commissioning artists is definitely outside our budget."

Her face fell. "That could be a problem. Unless . . ."

He could practically see the wheels turning in her head. "Unless what?"

She stopped mid-sidewalk to look up at him. "What about the high school? They have an art class, don't they?"

"Yeah. Kay Swinton still teaches it." A slow smile stretched across his face. "And Doug has asked me at least a dozen times if there was anything he and Kay could do to help with the project."

Hallie nodded. "He's asked me the same thing whenever I come into the bank."

Trey grinned. "I think we just found them a job. Do you think there's time?"

She paused, catching her bottom lip in her teeth. "We can give them three weeks. We're not looking for a Michelangelo. If they think the high school kids can produce something colorful in a Texas theme, I say we go for it."

"Risky." Visions of garishly colored childish scribbles ran through his mind. "Could be horrible."

She extended her arm toward the storefronts. "Not as horrible as these boards. Besides, a friend recently told me anything worthwhile involves some level of risk."

"He sounds very wise."

She gave him a playful shove. "Oh, he is. And *very* full of himself."

Trey chuckled and pulled open the door of Estelle's for Hallie to enter.

Smiling, Estelle greeted them from behind the cash register. "Your table is open in the back."

Hallie led the way, nodding at acquaintances while she walked to the booth against the wall. He waited until she slid onto her bench, the one facing the wall, before he took his place across from her.

Ten years ago, they would have sat side by side on his bench, holding hands under the cover of the table. He didn't have anything against hand-holding, but there was a lot to be said for sitting across from Hallie. He could look at her for hours, watching emotions play across her face. Her eyes were particularly expressive, dark and dancing with mischief one minute, lit with inspiration the next.

She caught him studying her and lifted a hand to her hair. "What?"

"I was just thinking how pretty you are." The honest words were out of his mouth before he could stop them.

He had to restrain the heel of his hand from slamming into his forehead. What am I doing?

"Yeah, right." She laughed as if he'd made a joke. "I see right through your ploy, Trey Gunther. What do you want?"

Playing along to save face, he lifted his palms in mock surrender. "Okay, you caught me. I was angling for you to contact Kay Swinton."

"I'll be happy to." She pulled a pad of paper from her bag, flipped it open, and made a note to herself. "I'll call her this afternoon and tell her what we're looking for."

Estelle arrived and took their order for two fried chicken dinners with mashed potatoes, butter beans, and corn.

"What's on the menu for dessert?" Hallie asked.

"Chocolate cream pie. I cut the pieces really big." Estelle shot Trey a sly wink. "I think you two will want to share."

She was clearly matchmaking. Oh great. Had she seen him staring at Hallie like a lovesick puppy and decided to help promote his cause? Man, he hoped he hadn't been that obvious. He needed to get himself together. Things were moving too fast.

He wasn't entirely sure what his feelings for Hallie were, but whatever they were, he had no intention of making them public.

He'd been down that road before. If he was going to crash and burn, it would be his secret. A man had his pride.

After Estelle left, Trey opened the folder he'd been carrying and angled it between them. "Here's the timeline for the sidewalks. According to the contractor, they will have everything done and cleaned up in three weeks. That's with a five-day margin in case of weather delays."

He pulled a calendar from underneath the timeline. "The construction on the gazebo should be done in two weeks. The electrician is on board to begin then. He anticipates it'll be a two-day job to get everything wired."

Hallie traced her finger along the calendar grid as he spoke, going out a week past the last projected completion date. She tapped the square with her pale pink nail. "Realistically, we can set the festival one month from Saturday."

"I think so. Even with adding the murals, everything should be completed by then."

She wrote the date, May 1, in her ever-present notebook. "Okay, once you run it by the chamber and council, I'll get the word out." She put down her pen and closed the book to give him her attention. "So, what was the big news you said you had for me about the festival committee? Don't tell me Miss Rose backed out. She sounded so excited about it."

"Nope. Rose is still 100 percent in. But when Etta Greely heard Rose was going to head the committee, she volunteered to serve as a cochair."

"That's nice." Hallie studied him for a moment and frowned. "What? Why do you have that pained expression on your face? Is there a problem?"

"I hope not." He leaned in and lowered his voice. "It's just that while Rose Meacham and Etta Greely are the best of friends, they can also be cutthroat competitors."

"Meaning?"

"Hopefully nothing. We'll just have to keep an eye out for a contest of one-upmanship. I know these women. It could get ugly."

Hallie sat back and laughed. "I'm sorry, but that's ridiculous. Mrs. Meacham and Mrs. Greely are two of the dearest ladies in town. I can't imagine them being cutthroat about anything. Get ugly?" She laughed again. "I'm sure they'll do just fine. You made it clear to them we want to keep this simple, right? A food booth and a couple of games for the kids. That's all."

"Yeah, they know." He rubbed his jaw. "I just think we need to be aware."

Hallie wagged her head and gave him a patronizing pat on the hand. "Poor Trey. I think the stress of the project is starting to get to you. Don't worry, everything will be just fine."

CHAPTER SIXTEEN

I t's started. Don't say I didn't try to warn you."
Hallie sat up in bed, clasping her cellphone to her ear. "Trey? What's started? What are you talking about?" She turned to squint at the clock on her nightstand. "And why are you calling me at 6:35 in the morning?"

"Oh, sorry, I wasn't even looking at the time. I just wanted to give you a heads-up. The escalation. It's begun."

"You are making no sense. I need caffeine." She swung her legs over the bed, pushed her feet into her fluffy slippers, and padded to the kitchen to fix a cup of coffee. "Now start at the beginning. What escalation are you talking about?"

"The ladies. Rose and Etta. They got wind of the fact that the high school art class has agreed to paint a mural for us. Rose figured if the art department could participate, then her high school choir should make a showing as well. She wants an hour during the festival for her choir to perform a program of patriotic songs."

Hallie clicked on the coffee maker she'd filled last night before going to bed. "News travels fast. I only talked to Kay about it yesterday." She opened the cabinet and pulled out a mug. "Oh, well, I guess we can fit them in."

"There's more. Etta's son teaches social studies at the high school. Apparently, his students recently created a project on the history of Village Green that Etta swears is professional quality. She wants us to use it as an exhibit at the festival."

She crossed to the table and sat. "What kind of project?"

"I'm not sure. We'll know more after we meet with Etta and her son up at the high school."

The smell of brewing coffee filled the small kitchen. "And we're meeting them *when*?"

"Noon. Today. Is Helen coming to see your mom?"

"Yes, I think so."

"Excellent. I'll pick you up at 11:30."

Hallie and Trey walked into the county high school a little before noon. They signed in at the reception desk, picked up their visitor badges, and headed toward the social studies classroom. Walking down the linoleum-tiled hall, past rows of dented metal lockers, brought back many memories, but she had a tough time recapturing even one of them because of the slight weight of Trey's hand at the small of her back. His touch distracted her.

She wrinkled her nose. Even his touch couldn't distract her from some things. "Isn't it strange that after all these years, the school still smells exactly the same?"

Trey inhaled noisily. "You're right. It still stinks."

They laughed, walked, and read the numbers over the doors. They stopped at the classroom at the far end of the hall. The door was open, and the desks were empty, so Trey ducked his head inside. "Hello? Anybody here?"

Etta bustled to the door to greet them with a broad smile. "Come in. Roger is grabbing a quick bite in the cafeteria. He told me to go ahead and show you the project. He'll join us in a minute."

They followed her to the back of the classroom. "Here it is." She swept her arm in a dramatic arc. "Isn't it just perfect?"

The project consisted of two dressmaker dummies, one clothed in a cotton dress and bonnet from the late 1800s. The second wore a dress and hat from the 1940s. Behind them, bullet points from the town's history were spread over six hand-lettered poster boards attached side by side to the wall.

Trey and Hallie exchanged a quick look. The assignment was clearly not festival-worthy. However, turning down any volunteered goods or service was particularly tricky. A perceived insult or slight could split the small town wide open. He nodded slightly, indicating he would take point.

"Mrs. Greely, this is a very impressive project." Trey stepped toward the mannequins to study them more closely. "I can tell the kids put a lot of work into it. But I'm just not sure how we could display it to full advantage."

She folded her arms and surveyed the project critically. "It needs more, doesn't it?"

"Well, ma'am—"

She lifted a palm to stop him. "You just leave it to me." She furrowed her brow and spoke, primarily to herself. "I know Eddie Bray has a couple of antique cars and a truck in the back of his garage we could use for the different decades. There's an old plow rusting in the field out by Helen West's place, and I have quilts going all the way back to my great-great-grandmother."

Hallie tried to gently inject some reality into the woman's fevered plotting. "We've set the date. May first. The festival will be in one month."

Etta glanced back at them, blinking as though she'd forgotten they were standing with her. "Give me a week. I'll put the word out and see what I can come up with to create some of those scenes you see at museums."

"Vignettes?"

"That's right." She looked at the poster boards. "The kids have our history broken down into six segments. I'll try to find something for each time period, for a total of six vignettes."

Hallie shook her head. "I don't know, Mrs. Greely. That sounds very ambitious for such a short amount of time."

Etta narrowed her eyes. "If Rose can do a concert—" She stopped herself and stretched her lips into a smile. "It's the least I can do."

The moment they were back in Trey's truck he turned to Hallie. "Do you think she can pull it off?"

"I don't know." Hallie frowned. "She looked determined. Scary determined."

"That's what I'm afraid of." He started the engine. "So, if, on the off chance she can scrape together enough stuff for six displays, where in the world would we put it? Doesn't sound like a good fit for the Green."

"I have a thought. The building at the corner of Main and Park used to be a car dealership, right?"

"Yeah."

She scrunched up her face to visualize the site. "Am I remembering correctly that it has glass windows facing both streets?"

He nodded. "That's right. It used to be the showroom."

"What's in there now?"

He took his eyes off the road just long enough to look at her and shrug. "I have no idea. Joe owns the building. We could ask him."

"That'll be your assignment. I'll text it to you so you'll remember." She pulled out her cell phone and typed in the message.

"While you're asking, would you see if he would be willing to let us use the space, temporarily, for our museum?"

Trey snorted. "A museum in a month? Really? And you thought Mrs. Greely was ambitious?"

Hallie grinned. "I think she's certifiable. But she gave me an idea. You and I were just talking about how bad downtown looks with all the boarded-up stores. What if we pulled the plywood off one store and built a series of smallish window displays inside it?"

She laughed at his wide-eyed expression of alarm. "Go with me on this. I'm thinking of department store windows. We wouldn't open the building to the public. People would view the vignettes from the street. We'd partition off three separate scenes down one side of the building, and three down the other. Since it was a car dealership, there must be a door wide enough to get big things, like Eddie's old cars, inside."

"You know you're crazy, right?"

The words weren't flattering, but delivered in a deep, silky purr with a look warm enough to melt her insides. She felt as though she'd been caressed. Heat stained her cheeks. "I thought you said I was positive and assertive."

"You are." He grinned and reached over to flick the ends of her hair. "Positively crazy."

Back at the bank, Hallie pulled up the festival page on the city website. Originally a several-paragraph blurb with a short description and the date and times of the event, it now covered a screen and a half. By necessity, the festival times had been expanded from the original eleven in the morning until noon to the current ten till five.

The schedule appeared as a spreadsheet, broken down into fifteen-minute increments so she could enter each attraction and when and where it would be held.

She scrolled down, adding the latest entry, a half-hour, gospel sing-along with a quartet from the church choir, between a roping exhibition by the FFA, and a performance by the preschoolers from Binky Warren's daycare. Done. Now every slot was full.

So much for keeping it small.

She'd complained good-naturedly to Trey about it, but truthfully, it was difficult not to get caught up in the energy. Village Green was all-in on the revitalization. As was the county. Since the high school served the whole area, kids from neighboring towns would participate in the festival. Which meant all their relatives would be on hand to watch the performances, taste the food, and see the sights.

She pulled out her trusty spiral-ring notebook and wrote a reminder to ask the food committee if they'd factored in family and friends to their estimates. While she was at it, she'd check to be certain the games group had plenty of prizes.

After saving changes to the website, Hallie moved to the city's Facebook page and added a post mentioning the latest update to the event programming. She subtracted another day from the motto contest countdown and clicked out of the account.

She flipped to a fresh page in her notebook and jotted a reminder to submit a festival schedule to the Fort Worth newspaper. Every Tuesday, the paper published a weekly calendar of events. It was a long shot to expect anyone to make the drive out from the city, but she couldn't pass up free publicity.

Her connections at *Texas Travels* had been beyond generous. In addition to the well-placed, two-page article they had published in this month's edition, they agreed to include quick updates on their website in the "What to Do This Weekend" section. It was difficult to track the article's impact, but hits on the city website continued to multiply.

Somebody was interested. Hallie prayed it was a lot of somebodies.

This weekend, the county bimonthly paper would debut the logo she and her graphic designer created for Village Green in a full-page ad. Integrated into the colorful artwork was a shadowy banner they would fill in later with the new town motto after the winner was announced.

Hallie smiled. Trey called her last night to say her motto submission was one of the ten selected by the nominating committee to be placed on the ballot. Major surprise.

Actually, the whole revitalization project had been one big surprise. From the moment she and Trey had been named cochairs, nothing had gone as she expected.

Her biggest concern had been juggling her public relations job with her commitment to the project. She'd anticipated a stressful month or so, trying to make things happen on two fronts and keeping both sets of clients happy. The stress hadn't materialized.

In fact, things had gone so smoothly, she wondered what she'd been doing with her time before the renovations. Her mornings were designated for company business. She fixed her mom an early breakfast, then disappeared into her bedroom for four hours of focused, uninterrupted work. At noon every day, she left the room, knowing she'd accomplished what she needed to do and had delegated the peripheral duties to her assistant. Funny, in their weekly progress meeting last week, they agreed the forced efficiency had made them both more productive.

Definitely unexpected. In a good way.

The fact Hallie hadn't yet locked down suitable living arrangements for her mother was also a surprise. The bad kind. She never dreamed it would take so long to get it resolved.

Yes, she had found a wonderful place for her mom. The bright and clean facility surpassed her exacting standards and would be a perfect place for her mother to live. No, her mother didn't know just how perfect it was because she refused to visit the site. The extent of her mother's stubbornness had been a major shock.

She sighed. She wanted her mother to be in full agreement with whatever arrangement they made. The idea of settling her without her approval was unthinkable. They may not get along, but Hallie loved her and wanted the best for her. She'd tried to be patient with her, giving her time to come to terms with reality. Unfortunately, time was running out.

Just yesterday she told her mom the day of the festival was decision day. If they couldn't agree on an acceptable living arrangement by then, Hallie would be moving her to the Nurture Assisted Living Center, with or without her consent. No surprise that her mother received the news with noisy tears and a bout of cane thumping.

Hallie stood and walked to the front window. She pushed aside the frilly curtain and looked out onto the street. Nothing had happened the way she expected.

From the moment she drove into town, antacids at the ready, she planned to stay far away from the community who had whittled her self-esteem into dust. Holing up at her mom's had worked for the previous decade. She saw no reason to change.

But when she stood up before the chamber and mayor's council and offered her suggestions, she'd unwittingly opened the door to constant interaction with the people she wanted to avoid. She had not foreseen the genuine pleasure she would derive from working side by side with them. She was stunned to discover she actually liked these people. They were quirky, a little crazy, and all too frequently up in her business, but she liked them.

It didn't hurt that since the revitalization project had been largely her idea, she had become something of a celebrity. Instead of cutting remarks, she got compliments. There were still the occasional unflattering comparisons to her near-perfect sister, but Hallie had chosen to forgive them.

The power of forgiveness had been a huge surprise.

After she'd made the decision to forgive, she'd experienced an immediate lightening of heart and spirit. It didn't take long to discover forgiveness was not a one-time decision, but a process. Each day, as a hurt surfaced, she had to choose again not to embrace it but to release it to God. And every time she released it, a bit of the bitterness she'd carried so long chipped away, freeing her heart to . . .

Freeing her heart to what?

Freeing her heart to love.

Of all the unexpected results of her return home, the biggest surprise was falling in love with Trey Gunther.

Hallie stepped away from the window and sucked in a breath. Until this moment, she hadn't allowed herself to fully acknowledge what her heart had been trying to tell her—she was in love with Trey.

She pressed her palms to heated cheeks. When had it happened? How had he penetrated her thick armor?

The more important question—what would she do with the knowledge?

She couldn't tell him. She rubbed a hand across her stomach. Just the thought of exposing her feelings to his rejection made her physically ill. No. She couldn't tell him. She didn't have that kind of courage.

But love, this bubbly truth that had been slowly inching its way through her heart and consciousness, would not be silenced. Even now, with the real fear he didn't share her feelings, she knew the words "I love you" would be on her tongue, waiting to spring out at the slightest provocation. A touch of his hand, a look in his eye, even his easy smile could trigger the spoken words.

Frantic thoughts ricocheted in her brain. She'd have to stay away from him. She'd have to keep her distance until she gained control over these new, exciting feelings.

Impossible. Over the next few days, they would be practically joined at the hip. With the festival just days away, she and Trey would spend every waking moment together—a thought which alternately thrilled and horrified her.

If she couldn't avoid him, she'd just have to be very careful.

She could do it. She could rein in her emotions, keeping a lid on the words waiting to spill out. She'd be vigilant, staying out of reach of his hands that rested so naturally on her back or shoulders. When he turned the full power of his gaze on her, she'd look away. And when his smile hit full wattage and her heart rhythm danced, she'd breathe slowly and focus on something else.

Hallie took a deep breath. Yes. She could do it. She could be careful and protect her fearful heart. But all the while, she'd be watching and listening, alert to any clue that just maybe—he loved her too.

Which would be the best surprise of all.

CHAPTER SEVENTEEN

Trey took the stairs two at a time at the Nichols's residence. He tapped twice on the screen door and let himself inside.

"Morning, ladies." He nodded to Hallie's mom and Helen. "Big day planned?"

Helen stood and approached him with a wide smile. "Can I get you something to drink while you're waiting for Hallie? She'll be ready in just a moment, but we've got coffee or iced tea if you'd like it."

"No, thank you. I've got drinks in the truck for later. Weatherman says it's going to get warm today."

Helen nodded. "That's just what I've been telling Leah. We're going to practice the stairs this morning, and I think we'll want to do it before it gets too hot."

Trey couldn't get over the change in Helen in a few short weeks. Gone was the shy woman with no confidence and little to say. Today she stood tall, met his eyes easily, and spoke with natural poise. Hallie told him that Helen said working with her mother had given her purpose. It was easy to see.

"I thought I heard you in here." Hallie breezed into the room in a pair of shorts and a T-shirt. She smiled up at him. "I'm ready when you are."

"Today is the big workday, isn't it?" Hallie's mother said. "Helen told me we can go to the Green this afternoon and see how everything looks."

"Better be careful, or we'll put you to work," Trey said.

The ladies were still giggling when he and Hallie walked out the front door.

Hallie waited for him on the top step, the sunlight shining off her hair. She slipped on a pair of sunglasses. "So, what's up first?"

"I've got a load of potting soil and flowers in the back of the truck. You and I are going to deliver them to the flowerpots that Joe's team has already distributed this morning."

They descended the stairs together. "What about the benches?"

He nodded. "We set them out last night. Have I mentioned to you how heavy they are?"

Hallie snorted. "Several times. I still think we made the right decision. Going with the sturdier construction will pay off in the long run."

"Says the woman who wasn't lifting them out of truck beds for two hours."

She snickered. "Aww. Poor baby."

He opened her door, standing close enough that when she passed him to climb into the cab, her subtle fragrance surrounded him. "You smell great."

She flashed him a smile before looking away. "Thanks. Soap is an amazing thing."

He chuckled, pushed her door shut, and rounded the truck to climb in on the other side. "Your mom and Helen looked like they were having fun."

"They were. I swear, I hear them laughing constantly. Like a couple of kids." She fastened her seat belt and turned to him. "I did speak to Helen about paying her for all the time she spends with

Mother. It took some convincing, but she finally agreed to accept a sitting fee."

He thought of the changes he'd witnessed in the Nichols's living room this morning. "I think helping with your mom has really benefitted her."

"I do too. It's been good for both of them. Hopefully after Mom moves to assisted living, Helen will consider taking a job somewhere as a caregiver. She's a natural."

"Is the assisted living thing a done deal?"

She nodded. "Yup. Saturday is D day. The saleslady at Nurture says they have an apartment coming open next week. I've arranged for Mom and me to go in on Monday and sign the papers. If everything goes according to plan, I'll have her moved in by Friday."

"I'll be glad to help you. We can haul her stuff in my truck, and I have access to a trailer if we need more space."

A brow appeared over the rim of her sunglasses. "The move will involve some heavy lifting. Will you be recovered from the benches, or do I need to call in some additional muscle?"

He laughed at the dig. "I think I can manage it."

She grinned. "Thank you."

"Is your mom good with all this?"

"Hard to say. She won't actually talk with me about it. She seems to think if she ignores the situation, it'll just go away." Hallie frowned. "If I try to press her about it, she cries. It's horrendous. But time's up. When the festival is over, my job here is done."

Trey had more in common with Mrs. Nichols than he thought. He'd been trying to ignore the fact Hallie would be leaving, hoping if he didn't acknowledge it, somehow she wouldn't go.

He didn't want her to leave. The last few weeks had been amazing. Maybe the best of his life. Spending time with Hallie, seeing her every day, had transformed him.

Everything was better. Brighter. He couldn't give her up. Once he'd experienced the richness of life with her by his side, he wasn't willing to let her go.

But how did he make her stay?

He knew she liked him. She'd mentioned more than once she considered him a friend. And that was a start. Especially considering their history. But friendship wouldn't keep her here.

Besides, his feelings for her went way beyond friendship. Friendship was tame. What he felt for her was powerful. All-consuming. Like nothing he'd ever known before, not even in their high school days.

He couldn't wait to spend time with her, to watch her, to listen to her, just to experience life alongside her. When he wasn't physically with her, he was thinking about her.

He had it bad.

The problem was he didn't think she did. She liked him, but did it go deeper? She enjoyed his company, but did she need it like he needed hers?

If he was any kind of man, he'd just ask her. He'd lay out his heart and let the chips fall.

Apparently, his man card was in jeopardy. Call it cowardice or just healthy self-preservation, but nothing would induce him to pour out his feelings to her.

He'd been down that road before. And her rejection had been unbearable. Beyond the worst pain he'd ever known. It had taken him years to recover.

Today, when the stakes were infinitely higher, rejection would be—no, he wouldn't go there. It didn't matter. Because he wasn't going to risk it.

So where did that leave him?

He was an optimist, right? He still had some time. He'd use these next few days to observe her, to gauge her reaction to him. If the opportunity arose, he'd steer the conversation to a state-of-the-relationship discussion. He'd get the information he needed and keep his pride intact.

He turned onto Main Street and pulled into a parking space a few feet from one of the enormous, cement flowerpots they'd purchased. "Here's the first one."

Hallie unbuckled her seatbelt and leaned forward for a better view. "They look great. Even better in person than online." She swallowed hard. "And bigger."

"They'll look fantastic with flowers in them. And they are heavy enough, nobody will mess with them." He switched off the engine. "Our job is to drop off the potting soil and plants. A separate crew will come around to fill the pots and plant the flowers."

Hallie tilted her head. "How do we know how many bags of dirt to leave? How many will it take to fill one of the pots?"

He tipped up his ball cap to study them. "Good question. Maybe we should fill the first one ourselves."

They lugged three twenty-pound bags from the truck. Trey cut open the first one and upended it into the pot. He peered inside. "Uh, oh. First twenty pounds didn't make a dent. I think we've got ourselves a black hole."

Hallie laughed and dragged the second bag to him. It took all of the third bag and half of a fourth to get the level of soil even with the concrete rim.

She stood, hands on her hips, studying the finished product. "Do we have enough for all ten pots?"

He shook his head. "We only have thirty bags. We'll need to make another run to the feed store."

She walked over to peer into the back of the truck. "The good news is I think we have plenty of flowers and ivy. I can climb in and choose the flowers and hand them down to you."

"Sure."

If he'd been any kind of gentleman, he'd have offered to climb into the truck bed, but he told himself she was probably better at picking flowers than he was. And he was honest enough to admit it wouldn't be a hardship to watch her up there at work. Shorts and a T-shirt were a good look on Hallie.

She selected a variety of plants in complementary shades and placed each of the four-inch pots into a plastic tray, then walked to the edge of the truck bed and handed the tray down to him. "Just look how beautiful these are."

He never took his eyes off her. "Probably the most beautiful thing I've ever seen."

Her gaze lifted to his for a fraction of a second, confirming he was talking about her and not the plants, then darted away. She cleared her throat. "After we've delivered all this stuff, and they've had a chance to get it planted, we should take a walk-through to get the full effect."

"Sounds like a plan."

It took over two hours to deliver the potting soil and plants they carried in the truck. After they picked up a second load of dirt from the feed store, they took a quick lunch break at Burger Bob's.

"That was delicious," Hallie said when they left the restaurant. "Thank you. I didn't realize how hungry I was."

"All that climbing in and out of the truck works up an appetite."

Hallie paused at the passenger door to roll her shoulders. "I think I'm going to feel all this lifting tomorrow."

"Aww, poor baby." Trey reached out, placed his hands on her slender shoulders and gently kneaded. "What you need is a massage."

He felt her lean into his hands, absorbing his touch with a sigh of pleasure. Suddenly, she stiffened before jerking away like she'd received an electric shock.

"Thanks. I'm good." She hopped up into the cab before he could lower his hands.

He was clearly moving too fast. Slow down, Gunther. You don't want to scare her off.

Trey had telephoned Ted Bixby, the team lead on the planting crew, to tell him which pots to start with while he and Hallie picked up the additional soil. By the time they got back to the bank where the final pots were located, the crew was waiting for them.

Trey dropped the tailgate, and he and Hallie climbed in to hand down the bags of soil to the volunteers. "Have you been here long?"

Mr. Bixby hoisted a bag onto his shoulder. "No, we just got here. We took an iced tea break a half hour ago. All this planting is thirsty work."

After the dirt was unloaded, Trey took Hallie's hand and helped her down from the truck bed. She dusted off her hands as she looked off in the direction of the completed pots. "How does it look so far?"

Mr. Bixby rocked back on his heels and grinned. "I'm real proud of it. The flowers add just the right amount of polish to things. You two will have to go take a peek for yourselves."

Trey looked at her. "What do you think? Are you ready to take a tour?"

She smiled and nodded. "Absolutely. Then I'm done. We've put in our time. I'm ready to head home for a shower."

They said their goodbyes to the crew and set off toward the Green. As they crossed the street and stepped up on the sidewalk bordering the park, it was not lost on Trey that this same route had been the catalyst for the whole revitalization project.

Hallie must have been thinking the same thing. "The new sidewalk makes all the difference."

He thought so too. It had cost a fortune, but it was money well spent. "I'm just glad we don't have to worry anymore about pets and small children disappearing into one of the cracks."

Hallie looked up at him and laughed. "It was awful, wasn't it? Remember, there was one hole so deep, I almost lost a shoe."

He knew he was in imminent danger of getting lost in those big brown eyes. He blinked. "What? Oh, yeah. I was so embarrassed when I noticed just how bad things had become around here. Our conversation at lunch that day launched all this. How does it feel to know you've changed everything?"

She lifted her shoulders in an easy shrug. "I know I didn't do it alone. You supplied the vision, and the town supplied the manpower."

A group of volunteers waved to them from the gazebo. "Trey! Hallie! Can you give us a hand with these pennants?"

Hallie sighed. "So much for my hot shower."

He wrapped an arm around her shoulder. "Sorry, kid. Duty calls."

They passed through the gate in the freshly painted iron fence onto the lawn of the Green.

Hallie paused. "It looks beautiful. I'm really glad we went with the flower beds instead of pots in here."

He stopped beside her, pushing up the brim of his ball cap to study the landscape. "You know, I've been optimistic about all this from the beginning, but if you had told me a month ago that Village Green would polish up to look like something out of a travel brochure, I'd have thought you were nuts. But look at this."

"It's amazing."

"It's a miracle." An honest-to-goodness miracle—the direct answer to his desperate prayer a few short weeks ago. His dilapidated town had been transformed, taking the first crucial steps from decay toward a new life of prosperity. His gaze swept the park. The transformation was everything he'd ever dreamed of and everything he'd been working toward since he took his place at the bank after college.

And at that moment, he'd trade it all for the woman beside him.

All the growth and hope for the future would be nothing without Hallie in his life.

Prayer swelled in his heart as they walked the gravel path to the gazebo. *Father, You have done all this—more than I could ever have asked or hoped for. When I see the beauty of this place, I am truly blown away by Your abundant provision. I'm so grateful. But there's a problem. My focus has been so narrow that I almost missed the most important thing. Lord, I need Hallie. And for that I'm going to need another miracle.*

They worked alongside the volunteers until well past dark, and by the time Trey drove Hallie home, they were both filthy and exhausted. He was particularly disappointed that not once over the busy afternoon or evening did they have the opportunity to speak privately.

Time was running out. One week from today was the festival. She'd get her mother settled, then she'd be gone. Something told him once she returned to her life and friends in Fort Worth, she'd be lost to him.

"You know, maybe staying here wouldn't be such a bad thing." He kept his tone casual, as though the thought had just occurred to him. "Village Green needs people like you."

He snuck a peek out of the corner of his eye to catch her reaction.

She leaned against the headrest, her eyes closed. "Village Green needs people. Period."

"Well, yeah." He waited a beat, then tried again. "It's really not a bad little town. We've got a lot of history. And it's safe and friendly—"

Head still propped on the headrest, she turned slightly to flash him a weary smile. "I wrote the brochure, remember?"

His chuckle sounded awkward. "I remember. I was just reminding you. In case, you know, staying ever went through your mind."

"I've thought about it—"

Past tense. Not good. Rising panic had him interrupting her. "—the only reason I'm bringing it up is that this revitalization is only the beginning. To continue attracting visitors, we'll need to provide reasons for them to come." His mouth was just running, saying anything that came to mind. "Maybe something at Christmas. We could use your expertise to keep the ball rolling."

She turned away and closed her eyes again. "Now that you've done it once, I think you'll find the basic framework will be the same. And if you get in a bind, I'll only be a phone call away."

CHAPTER EIGHTEEN

Hallie's mother walked into the kitchen, her cane tapping lightly on the pebbled linoleum, and made her way to the table. "Today's the big day."

"Yes, ma'am." Hallie pulled out a chair and helped her mom settle in. "The festival starts in just a few hours."

"Well, that too." Her mother's expression seemed unusually determined. Even cheerful. "Aren't you going to ask me where I've decided to live?"

Hallie's heart sank. Today was the agreed upon decision day, but she didn't want to have this discussion now. She hadn't had her first cup of coffee yet, and she didn't want to start what she knew would be a long day with an argument. She walked to the counter and poured them both a cup. "Why don't we wait and talk—"

"I'm going to stay right here."

Hallie sagged against the cabinet. She sighed and shook her head. "No, Mom. We've already talked about this. You can't stay here. I've got to go back to Fort Worth, and you can't live here by yourself. It won't work. It's possible that one day you'll be able to live independently, but right now, you need assistance."

"Helen can help me."

She carried the drinks to the table, handed one to her mom, and sat beside her. "Helen is a wonderful friend, and I hope she'll visit you often at the assisted living center."

Her mother shook her head. "No. I'm not moving to an assisted living center. It's all decided. Helen is going to move in here with me."

"She what?" Hallie was glad she was sitting down. "Since when?"

"We've been discussing it for the last week or so. It's the perfect solution for all of us. Helen can't afford her farm. She's decided to sell it and move into town. She needs to find a job and a place to live. I need a caregiver, at least for now, and we have plenty of room in the house. It's not like Janice is going to move back."

Hallie's eyes widened. Her mom had progressed further than she'd thought. "No, I think she's pretty committed to Bubba."

Her mother ignored the sarcasm. "Helen and I are great together. She enjoys helping me, and I love having her around. And we are both tired of being lonely."

Hallie smiled and laid her hand over her mom's. "You two do make a wonderful team. But I've looked at the numbers. Even with the modest salary we're paying her, we can't afford to have her twenty-four hours a day."

Her mother nodded. "We talked about that. We can pay her for twelve hours a day, and the other twelve hours she'll collect in room and board. The money she'll be saving by not paying rent and utilities and buying food will more than compensate for the other half of her salary."

Hallie's head spun with the possibilities. Her mother could stay in her home and have a full-time caregiver. The best of both worlds. "This could work."

"Helen planned to talk with you about it today, but it's just so exciting, I couldn't wait."

When Helen arrived to speak with Hallie an hour later, it was easy to see she was equally excited. Her eyes sparkled as she spoke. "I've been praying about what to do now that Elmer's gone. Living with Leah and taking care of her is a direct answer to my prayer. I'll be able to stay in Village Green with the people I know, and I'll have meaningful work. Even better, we'll have each other for company."

Hallie took her hands and waited until she had Helen's full attention. "I love this idea. I can't think of anyone I'd rather have here than you. But I have to ask. What if—"

Helen nodded. "I know what you're going to say. What if it doesn't work out? Leah and I have been very frank with each other. We don't foresee any problems, but we have agreed to a six-month trial period. If, at the end of that time, either of us feels the arrangement is not working, then we will look at alternatives."

Hallie drove into town in a blissful daze. The problem she couldn't unravel had solved itself. With some obvious divine intervention.

Now, if only God would step in and fix things with Trey.

Since she'd been home, they'd fallen into a fun, easy friendship, much richer than the one they'd shared in high school. Now she could see that she'd been so insecure back then that she'd related to him more like a fan worshipping an idol. He'd been everything she wasn't—confident, popular, and good looking, and she'd been awed and honored he'd even noticed her. She hadn't felt worthy of his attention and didn't believe deep down she could hold it.

Which, of course, she hadn't.

Today they interacted on a more even footing. She'd never be as attractive as he was. The man was criminally good looking, for heaven's sake, but she'd gained enough confidence in herself over the last decade that she could view him as a peer. She had something valuable to contribute to the relationship. The new friendship had a balance that made it stronger.

It was pretty clear he was attracted to her. Several times she'd caught him looking at her with a gaze so heated she wondered why she hadn't spontaneously combusted. But attraction was superficial. They'd been attracted ten years ago, and it hadn't been enough.

She wanted more. She wanted his heart. She wanted his love and devotion, not his gratitude for her service to his town. She wanted to hear him ask her to stay because being away from her would be agony, not because the town would need her direction in the future.

She knew he loved the town. Could he love her too?

Obviously, she needed a miracle. And soon.

Once the festival was over and Helen moved in with her mother, there was no good reason for her to hang around. Everyone knew her life and work were back in Fort Worth.

Just for today, however, she was willing to postpone her personal miracle so God could direct His full attention to Village Green. They'd really gone out on a limb for the festival, put in so much time and money, and they needed heavenly backup to make the day a success.

Hallie parked on a side street to save prime spots for festival traffic. The forecast called for sunny in the mid-eighties, so she'd gone with a sundress and cute wedge sandals, hoping for an "I may be in charge, but I'm here to have a good time" kind of look. In the event the wedges interfered with her good time, she had a pair of sensible sneakers stashed in the back seat.

She climbed out of the car and locked it before heading to the Green. *"Okay, Lord. Show us Your stuff."*

His Hallie radar running full throttle, Trey sensed her before he saw her coming from a block away. He excused himself from the group gathered at the foot of the gazebo and jogged through the grass and across the street to join her.

"Good morning!" His eyes traveled from her head to her feet. "Wow. You look spectacular."

A pretty pink that matched the color of her dress suffused her cheeks. She lowered her eyes. "Thank you."

He fell into step beside her. Suddenly tongue-tied, like a thirteen-year-old with his first crush, he racked his addled brain for something to say. His gaze darted around, finally settling on the brightly painted boards hanging on the storefront beside them. "The kids really outdid themselves on the mural."

Hallie glanced up at the painting. "I love it. Who knew high school kids were that talented?"

"Dad said the chamber liked the mural and Mrs. Greely's 'history museum' so much they've decided to keep them as an ongoing exhibit. At least, until there's a new tenant."

His stomach clenched. Would there be new tenants? Would all the painting, polishing, and planting bear fruit? He held no delusions that the festival would kick off a meteoric rush of growth and prosperity. They were still off-the-beaten-path, small-town Texas. The things they'd accomplished so far were only the preliminaries, a foundation on which Village Green could slowly build toward a stronger future.

"Nervous?"

She must have sensed his mood. He lifted his shoulders. "A little. I have no doubt the festival will be a huge success. But what about tomorrow? And the next day? We've put so much into the revitalization, and now, the test. Will it work? Can we turn Village Green around?"

She laid a hand on his arm and gave it a squeeze, a friendly gesture that quieted the circling doubts and reminded him he wasn't in this alone. "I guess we wait and see. I'm hopeful. Everything looks great, and the whole town is totally onboard. It's a solid beginning."

He stopped to look down at her. "You know, I've said this before, but we couldn't have done this without you. I am more grateful to you than I can say."

She flashed him a smile. "I'm glad I could help. But honestly, it took someone to care enough." They continued toward the festival. "It was your devotion and determination that ultimately brought this together."

He was devoted to the town. In the interest of full disclosure, he needed her to see, to truly understand, that the welfare of Village Green, this tiny dot in the middle of nowhere, would always hold an important place in his life. He belonged here. It had been a significant stumbling block to their relationship in the past. Were they beyond it now?

Because for him, it was truly a matter of love me, love my town.

"I'd do anything for this place."

She met his eyes, and he could swear her smile dimmed. "Yeah, I get that."

When they arrived at the Green, he and Hallie were separated almost immediately. Though they were not the official festival chairs, if a question or problem surfaced, it was ultimately directed to them. She was dragged off to settle an issue in the food tents, while the mayor questioned him about the PA system.

Promptly at ten o'clock, Mayor Sellers took his place at the gazebo to kick off the festivities. The sun shone warm and bright on the hundred or so people gathered on the Green; not a cloud in the bright blue sky threatened the day's activities. The hundreds of multicolored pennants they'd spent all yesterday afternoon hanging rustled and snapped in the breeze. The sounds of kids laughing and the smells of fair food filled the air.

After the mayor made his welcome speech, Pastor Dale took the microphone to pray. The assembled group went respectfully silent while he thanked God for Village Green and asked His blessing on the day and all the participants. When he closed with an amen, the Green erupted with cheers and applause. Excitement and expectation were thick in the air. Trey's eyes met Hallie's across the thirty feet separating them. She shot him a big smile and a thumbs up.

He exhaled a deep breath to ease a sudden burst of tension. Everything was go. Let the festival begin.

After the first performers took their places on the gazebo, Trey walked over to the food tent to find Hallie. He had a responsibility to oversee the events, but there was no reason he couldn't combine pleasure with business.

She stood behind one of the six-foot tables that served as a border delineating the workspace, as well as a counter to display the individually wrapped, homemade food items for sale. She'd added an apron over her pink dress, and her thick brown hair was caught back in a ponytail.

Her eyes danced when she smiled up at him. "Hello, sir. What can I get you?"

An answering smile curved his mouth. "An hour of your time. I thought we could walk the Green and see how the first annual spring festival is going."

She frowned and shook her head. "Sorry. Turns out we're a little shorthanded in the food booth right now. I told them I'd help out."

He felt his face fall, his disappointment disproportionate to the situation. Today, of all days, he didn't want to share her. This was their time. Their party.

He shoved his hands in his pockets. "Oh. That was nice of you to volunteer."

"If you're free, check back later. Things may quiet down, and they won't need me anymore."

"Okay." He turned to go.

"Wait. You can't leave empty-handed. It's bad for business." She passed him a napkin with a big, golden muffin studded with blueberries and topped with sugary crumbs. As he reached for his wallet, she winked and shook her head. "It's on the house. See you in a bit."

He stepped away, cheered by her smile and the promise of her company later. He looked out over the park and munched on the muffin. He wasn't certain, but it appeared as though the crowd on the Green had already grown from when the festival first opened. Good sign. He headed over to a gate in the fence, exited the Green, and continued for a block until he reached Sam in the middle of the street directing traffic.

"What do you think, officer?" Trey chuckled. "Can Village Green's finest handle this mob?"

Sam signaled to the cars to proceed and crossed to the sidewalk where Trey stood. He gestured toward the road. "This is something, isn't it? I can't tell you the last time I saw this many cars in Village Green." He pushed back his hat to scratch his head. "Actually, I've never seen this much traffic in town. My deputy just radioed that the on-street parking downtown is completely full and the church lot is filling fast. We're going to start directing people to parallel park along the residential areas and walk to the Green. Somebody must have been listening to all that promotion your girlfriend's been doing."

Trey nodded. "Looks like. And she's not my girlfriend." Yet.

"I don't know what you're waiting for. It's obvious you're caught. That goofy look you get on your face when you see her is enough to give me sugar shock." Sam shuddered.

Trey snorted. "Sugar shock in a man who eats donuts breakfast, lunch, and dinner? Is that even possible?"

Sam grinned. "If it's not, it should be. Anyway, get on with it. And while you're at it, ask Hallie if she's got any good-looking friends she can recommend for me. Romantic prospects are pretty slim in our little corner of paradise."

He gave Trey a friendly shove and walked back out into the street to direct traffic. "Hey," he called. "Next time you come by, bring me something to eat, will you? I'm starving."

"Sure. What do you want?"

"Some of whatever it was you've got spilled down the front of you would be fine."

Trey laughed. "It's a deal." He brushed the half dozen crumbs off the front of his shirt and continued down to the next block. He crossed in front of the old automobile dealership to look at the history exhibit they'd pieced together behind the glass panes. Joe stood in front of it, hands in pockets, studying the windows.

Trey extended his hand. "I'm surprised to find you here. I don't remember you being interested in the history of Village Green, even when we had to know it for a test."

Joe sent him a look of pure horror. "I am not even remotely interested in the history of this godforsaken place." He turned his attention back to the store window. "I'm strictly here to admire the incredible craftmanship of the genius who built the framework and walls for these displays."

Trey laughed. "You did a great job. It looks sharp. Really professional."

"Your lady friend wouldn't accept any less." Joe tipped up a shoulder. "She's a tough taskmaster."

"You're just miffed because she wouldn't flirt with you."

Joe grinned. "Yeah, maybe. For some unexplainable reason, she seems to prefer you."

Please, God. Let it be true. "If she does, it's because she's a woman of taste and refinement."

"Or," Joe continued with feigned confusion, "it's because she has an unnatural attraction to men in loafers."

Trey was used to his friends ribbing about his conservative attire. "I'm a banker. Loafers come with the territory." He looked down at his friend's feet. "Maybe you should try a pair. See if you can up your game with the ladies."

Joe glanced at his sneakers. "Man, my game is already so good, I have to wear running shoes to keep from getting caught." He looked past Trey's shoulder and grimaced. "Oh, no. Here comes old lady Greely. Looks like she's leading a tour to her 'museum.' Time to put these shoes to use. I've had to listen to her spiel at least a dozen times while I was building those sets. No way I'm doing it again. There's only so much a man can take." He slapped Trey on the back before loping off in the opposite direction. "Catch you later."

Trey couldn't run since Mrs. Greely had seen him, but he wasn't willing to get trapped in her thirty-minute history lecture either. He whipped out his cellphone and pressed it to his ear as though he were engaged in an important conversation and walked briskly toward her group, passing them on the sidewalk with a smile and a nod. Once safely beyond them, he slowed his pace, checked the time on his phone, and stuffed it back in his pocket. It had been thirty-seven minutes since he'd left the food tent. He wondered if Hallie was free yet.

She'd looked relaxed and happy this morning. Like she was enjoying herself. He'd been waiting for the right moment to talk with her. To find out where they stood. To see if she would be willing to make his town her town. Maybe they could talk about it over lunch.

He ought to wait at least an hour before he dropped in on her again. He forced himself to walk slowly along Main Street, to study his newly revitalized town objectively. The transformation amazed him. The flowerpots and benches added color and the slow-down-and-take-a-moment feel they'd been aiming for. The exposed windows of empty storefronts had been scrubbed and de-grimed until sunlight reflected off the crystal clear panes. Joe and his crew had sanded the peeling paint from the buildings along Main Street and repainted both the street-level trim and the apartments above. Even the boarded-up stores, with their newly painted murals, looked fresh.

Beyond the city improvements, many of the business owners invested heavily in the future. Chet Wilke had hung a fancy new sign over his pharmacy and converted the front of his store into a gift shop. Estelle put up new awnings and had the name of her restaurant repainted on the windows in a frilly, old-timey font. Even the Grocery Giant got in the game with new signs over the entrances and a dozen new grocery carts.

His stomach did a nervous spasm. *Please, God, let their investment pay off. Bring people to our community. And can one of those people be Hallie? Because without her, all this is going to feel pretty empty.*

"Here he comes again." Mrs. Ryder's bracelets jangled when she elbowed Hallie. "That man must be powerful fond of our cooking."

Hallie smiled. Her heart swelled a little every time she realized handsome Trey Gunther was looking for her. She couldn't help but be flattered he'd come by at least once an hour to ask her to check out the festival with him. Unfortunately, each time she'd had to say no. The food concession had been slammed since they opened at ten, and she couldn't possibly leave. Even now, they were three deep at the tables with requests for drinks and snacks and the burgers that a couple of the church men were grilling out behind the tent.

She shook her head before he could ask. "I'm sorry, Trey. No break for me. I think we'd better assume I'm trapped here until we close it down."

His disappointment was clear. "Aw, Hallie, I hate for you to miss everything when you've worked so hard to bring it all together."

She smiled and shrugged. "It's okay. I've had a lot of fun, and we can hear the entertainment back here. I can't really tell since I haven't been out from behind the tables all day, but from the number of sodas I've poured, we must have a pretty good crowd."

He nodded. "Sam says parking is at capacity. Next festival he wants to run a shuttle from the high school so people can park there."

"Next festival?" She thought about her aching feet. "I'm not sure I'll survive this one."

He leaned across the table and lowered his voice. "You've got to. We have big plans to make."

A man elbowed up beside Trey. "Ma'am, can I get two lemonades, please?"

"Sure, coming right up." She flashed Trey an apologetic smile. "I've got to get back to work. I'll talk to you later."

CHAPTER NINETEEN

They didn't close down the food tent so much as simply run out of food. By four o'clock there wasn't a Rice Krispies treat or a drop of grape soda to be found. Hallie wrote CLOSED in big letters on the side of an empty cardboard box and placed it on the table.

"Thank heaven." Mrs. Ryder flopped down in one of the folding chairs set up inside the food prep area. "I don't think I have the strength to scoop one more bag of popcorn. Come sit down, Hallie. The cleanup can wait just a minute more. I've got to give these poor feet a rest."

Hallie took the chair beside her and pried off her sticky food-handling gloves. "I'm half afraid that if I sit down, I won't be able to get back up. It's a toss-up as to whether it would be because my legs are too tired to lift me or because I've stuck to the seat in festival food goo."

Mrs. Ryder laughed, reached over, and patted Hallie's shoulder. "You've put in a good day's work, honey. I don't know what we'd have done without you."

The other two women, older ladies from her mother's Sunday school class who'd manned the concession with them, agreed. "Next time we do this, we need to schedule more workers."

Mrs. Ryder snorted. "Next time we do this, I'm going to be on vacation somewhere far away."

They all laughed, the tired yet satisfied laugh of women who knew they'd served well.

"How much do you think we made?"

Mrs. Ryder shrugged. "Mason and Chet will count the till tonight. I bet they'll announce the totals at church tomorrow."

Hallie thought for a moment. "I'm sure it covered the cost of food, especially since most of it was donated, and the rest of it will go toward any expenses the town incurred for the festival."

"It's all been wonderful. The revitalization, the festival, everything," Mrs. Ryder said. "I'm just amazed at what the town accomplished in such a short time. And Hallie, most of the credit belongs to you."

The ladies nodded their agreement.

Hallie shook her head. "No, really the credit should go to Trey. He had the vision to improve Village Green. He's the one who believed the town could be so much more."

"Well, I say the two of you make a good team." Mrs. Ryder waggled her eyebrows. "Mason told me Trey can't talk without mentioning how grateful he is to you."

Grateful. Hallie was beginning to hate the word. Gratitude was miles away from the love she was looking for.

She stood and massaged her lower back. "Let's get this packed up. I'm ready to go home and soak off the sticky soda film that seems to be covering my entire body."

Mrs. Ryder got up with a groan. "I plan to sit in a bathtub up to my neck in hot water until my wrinkles get wrinkles."

The food tent had been set up about the length of a small parking lot away from the gazebo so they would have access to electricity. The proximity to the stage meant the concession workers could hear most of what transpired during the day. Now, they could hear the applause as the last act completed their performance, then the mayor's voice as he made some closing remarks.

Hallie was packing supplies into cardboard boxes when she thought she heard her name being called.

"Hey, Hallie, that's you." Mrs. Ryder tapped her on the shoulder. "The mayor just called your name."

Hallie looked up from the half-filled box. "Why?"

"I don't know, but he's asking you to come up on stage." Mrs. Ryder took the box of straws from Hallie's hand. "Go on."

The other ladies nodded and gestured for her to go.

She walked hesitantly from the tent, looking back over her shoulder at the ladies before stepping into the crowd gathered at the foot of the gazebo. A path opened for her to pass through, and she climbed the stairs to a semicircle of smiling people waiting for her at the top.

"Here she is," Mayor Sellers announced. He chuckled. "Bless her heart, our Hallie has been working so hard, she hasn't had the time to remove her apron."

The mayor's teasing remark elicited a laugh from the crowd. Hallie chose to laugh along with them rather than go with her initial reaction to shrink into her shoulders and cry.

He extended his hand that wasn't holding the microphone to her. "Turn around, Hallie. I want the folks to see you."

She turned to face the horrifyingly large audience and tried for a smile. She didn't need a mirror to know at least half of her hair had escaped her ponytail and was straggling down around her ears. She was covered in a layer of sticky concession crud and sporting a dowdy apron splattered with who-knew-what in front of the entire town.

How nice.

To top off her humiliation, she'd hardly had a chance to register who all was standing on the gazebo before she was forced to turn her back to them, but she had the crazy impression that her sister Janice was one of the people in the group.

Mayor Sellers wrapped a chummy arm around her shoulders. "As you know, the chamber sponsored a competition to create a motto for our town. Our panel of judges was asked to select the ten mottos that best represented Village Green and place them on a ballot for us to vote on. This past Wednesday, our judges tallied the votes and Hallie's submission 'The Place Where You Belong' won with a commanding majority of the votes."

The audience burst into excited chatter and applause.

"Even as I speak, a team from Allied Sign Company is replacing the sign at the city limits with a new one that reads, 'Welcome to Village Green, The Place Where You Belong'."

The applause grew louder. The mayor shook her hand. "Congratulations, Hallie." She hoped he didn't notice her fingers stuck a little bit to his when he released her.

Mayor Sellers faced the assembled group again. "Today has been a big day for our little town, and it's about to get bigger with a special presentation from one of our most illustrious past residents. I'm going to hand off the microphone to Trey Gunther and ask him to make the introductions."

Uncertain where she belonged in all the hoopla and determined to escape the spotlight, Hallie scuttled to the back of the group when Trey moved to the front center of the gazebo with Janice and her husband at his side.

"I know you all remember Janice Carson, formerly Janice Nichols. She and her husband, Coach Bubba Carson, drove in from west Texas to join us for the festival today. Thank you both for coming."

Hallie couldn't help but be proud of her older sister. She looked particularly lovely in a slim, blue sundress the exact color of her eyes and a pair of spiky sandals. Perfect hair, perfect makeup, perfect girl. Her innate poise made Hallie's long-practiced efforts look clumsy.

Maybe it was exhaustion talking, but Hallie realized the lopsided comparisons she'd chafed against all her life were absolutely true.

She would never measure up to her sister.

Janice eagerly took the mike. "We wouldn't miss it, Trey." She swung around to face the crowd. "Even though we're far away, we've kept up with all the exciting things happening in town through your website and Facebook page. Because of our busy schedules, we haven't been able to participate in the workdays, but Bubba and I wanted to do something to give back to this wonderful community."

Applause swelled.

"We decided to dig deep and contribute ten thousand dollars to Village Green to be used in whatever way the city deems best to make our town great again."

The crowd went wild. Shouts and clapping and whistling filled the air. Beaming like a homecoming queen, Janice pulled a check from her purse and presented it to Trey. She leaned into him for an impulsive hug, whispered something in his ear, then pressed a quick kiss to his cheek before stepping back beside her husband.

"Wow. Thank you." Trey faced Janice and Bubba and lifted the check. "This is incredibly generous. On behalf of the whole town, thank you both so much."

Hallie didn't hear another word. The innocent embrace and kiss catapulted her back to the life-shattering night she saw her sister and Trey kissing on the very same spot. Insecure eighteen-year-old Hallie's worst fears had been confirmed in that moment. She had not been good enough to hold Trey's love.

Twenty-eight-year-old Hallie had come a long way. She'd accomplished so many things she was proud of. Better yet, she was actively working to forgive the hurts of her past, pressing on to an unencumbered future. But buried deep down, deeper than any newfound confidence, lurked the fear she still wasn't worthy of his love.

The longer she stood there, the more embarrassed she became. What a fool she'd been. She'd built up these last few weeks of forced companionship with Trey into a fairytale.

Working side by side with him had definitely worn down the barriers from the last decade. They'd found respect for each other. She could honestly say they were friends.

She had been the one to read more into the friendship. She knew from observation Trey was a toucher—a hand on the shoulder, a pat on the back—he related to others by touch. Instead of applying that understanding to their relationship, she'd assigned special meaning to the times he'd rested a hand on her back or shoulder.

Trey had been born charming. She knew that. So why had she suddenly seen his charm as a reaction to her alone?

She knew she hadn't imagined that he enjoyed being with her. The look of pleasure on his face when they were together was unmistakable. But she also knew he used their time together to pick her brain about ways to promote his town. He needed her knowledge. He'd been incredibly honest with her. Even today, he'd made a point to remind her he'd do anything for Village Green.

Trey was grateful to her. But she wanted love, the same intense rush of emotion she experienced every time she saw him.

At least in all her stupid imaginings, she hadn't allowed herself to blurt out the truth. She may not have his love, but she'd been spared the embarrassment of expressing her unrequited feelings to him. That small satisfaction would have to be enough.

It wasn't difficult to escape the gazebo unnoticed. Janice's announcement had whipped the gathered crowd into an excited frenzy. Hallie passed through the friends and well-wishers climbing the stairs to greet Janice and her husband and made her way to her car unseen.

Back at the house, Hallie showered until there wasn't a drop of hot water left, successfully removing the grime of the long day. Though the steamy water couldn't rinse away the heavy sorrow of her heart, it did bring clarity to her mind.

She dried off with a towel. Time to go.

She'd come home to arrange care for her mother. Hiring Helen as caregiver was the perfect solution. A win-win for everyone. Since they'd agreed Helen would move in tomorrow after church, there was no reason for Hallie to stay.

She checked her cell phone before climbing into bed. Two texts. One from her sister, one from Trey. Janice's message said she hated to miss talking with Hallie, but she and Bubba had to get back tonight. She'd call later in the week, and they'd chat.

Trey's message was short. Where are you?

She texted her response. Exhausted. Showered and off to bed. We'll talk tomorrow.

Maybe by then she'd think of something to say.

CHAPTER TWENTY

I don't see why you aren't coming to church with us." Her mother's expression bordered on a pout. "There's no reason you need to leave so early."

Hallie focused on her coffee cup because it was easier to lie to an inanimate object. "I've been gone so long, it'll take me most of the day to get caught up with stuff around the apartment before I go back to work tomorrow."

"Why do you have to go at all? You can live here with Helen and me. It would be fun."

She lifted her gaze to her mother's and smiled. "It *would* be fun. But it's time for me to get back home. I don't belong here."

Her mother straightened. "Of course you do. Wasn't that your motto they are painting on the signs? 'Village Green, the Place Where *You* Belong'."

Hallie laughed. "Yes, it's my motto. But I wrote it as publicity for the town, not a personal credo."

"Don't you like it here?" her mother asked in an injured tone.

Hallie thought a moment. "I do like it here. Village Green is a wonderful place. With wonderful people. I'll be back to visit."

"When?"

"Often." She stood and pressed a kiss to her mother's forehead. "I promise."

Helen brought a load of her belongings when she came to pick up Hallie's mother for church. Hallie helped her carry them inside and place them in Janice's old room. The fact that her mother allowed Helen to take up residence in that exalted place was one more indicator of her high esteem.

Hallie held an armful of garments while Helen took them from her, one at a time, and hung them in the walk-in closet. "I'm so sorry you are leaving already," Helen said. "I hope you don't feel you have to hurry off because I'm moving in."

Hallie shook her head. "Not at all. I just need to get home."

Helen scanned her face for a moment, perhaps looking for an explanation for her sudden departure. "Your mother and I, Trey— we'll miss you."

"I'll miss you too."

Helen studied her again and pulled Hallie into a big hug. "Don't be a stranger. Your mother and I have already begun planning girlfriend weekends for the three of us."

After another round of hugs and promises to call and visit, Hallie loaded the two of them into Helen's car and sent them off to church. She waved them down the driveway before reentering the house to finish packing.

It didn't take long to place everything into her suitcases. As she carefully folded each item, she remembered how she'd felt the day she'd packed them to come to Village Green. She'd been scared for her mother and the unknown future, resentful she had to interrupt her busy life when her sister couldn't be bothered, and nervous about facing the ghosts of her past.

She zipped the suitcase closed and sat beside it on the bed, smoothing the coverlet with her hand. Today, her mother's future looked bright, her prognosis excellent. Hallie had found a measure of peace with her sister and the past. They hadn't changed, but through God's prompting and the process of forgiveness, Hallie's perception had been radically altered.

She'd never realized the emotional weight of the baggage she'd carried all those years or how by holding on to it, she'd actually been handicapping her own future. Though she still had a long way to go, she was proud to leave a stronger, wiser woman.

Hallie pushed off the bed with a sigh. Time to go. She took one last look around the little pink room, gathered her suitcases and laptop, and headed out.

She stopped halfway down the front steps to adjust her grip on the suitcases. She'd forgotten how heavy they were until she remembered she hadn't carried them up all those stairs when she arrived. Trey had. She hefted them into the trunk of her car and slammed the lid.

Climbing into the driver's seat, she paused and looked up at the house one last time. It had been a good visit. She wouldn't trade any part of it. Even her time with Trey.

He'd be looking for her at church this morning, eager to report on the success of the festival. She'd have to call him when she got back to Fort Worth. She sighed as she started the engine. She hadn't left town yet, and she already missed him. Talking to him and seeing him every day had become such an important part of her life. The best part.

She wouldn't regret falling in love with him. Honestly, how could she have prevented it? He was kind and funny and smart and compassionate and—well, she could spend the entire drive home reminding herself of all the reasons she loved him. Which would be incredibly stupid. No, now it was time to convince herself she was satisfied to be his friend.

And maybe in another decade, she'd believe it.

Trey had slept badly. The niggling unease he'd felt when he'd discovered Hallie had left the festival without talking to him had grown into full-on panic. Something was wrong.

He arrived at the church earlier than usual, unlocked the doors, set up the classrooms, and started the coffee. He walked to the sanctuary and sat in his customary place on the front pew. Too preoccupied to pray, he tried instead to find order in the churning chaos of his mind.

Fear muddled his thoughts. He massaged his eyes with the heels of his hands. *Come on, Gunther, get it together.*

He'd feel more confident if he had a plan. Bottom line, he needed to talk to Hallie ASAP. He'd take her to lunch, chat about the festival for a few minutes, then he'd ask her some leading questions to find out where her heart was. The most important thing— she had to go first. He refused to put himself out there, wouldn't expose his vulnerability as he'd done ten years ago when he'd begged her to stay.

Still fidgety, he left the sanctuary and went to the kitchen to fix himself coffee. He was on his second cup when Pastor Dale arrived.

"I bet you're on top of the world after yesterday's big success."

Trey stood and shook his hand. "Yes and no. I'm pumped about the festival. I think everyone had a good time, and the town got some excellent exposure."

Pastor waited and when Trey didn't continue, he walked over to the counter and picked up a Styrofoam cup. "Okay, I get the yes part, but I'm missing the no."

"Now that the festival is over, Hallie will be leaving." He turned his gaze to his cup. "I'm going to try to talk her into staying."

The pastor nodded and poured coffee from the dispenser. "That's not entirely unexpected. She'd make a wonderful addition to our town."

"It's more than that." Trey took a deep breath. "I love her."

Dale didn't appear surprised by Trey's confession. "Ahh. And does she know your feelings? Does she know you love her?"

"Not yet. I wanted to give it some time." Who was he kidding? This was his friend, the person with whom he could share his deepest thoughts. "Honestly, I wanted to know how she felt first. She stomped all over my heart ten years ago and shredded my pride." He blew out a breath. "It was brutal. I just can't go through that again."

"So, you are playing it safe. Protecting your Gunther pride."

"No, that's not . . ." His denial rang hollow. Probably because that was exactly what he was doing. "Yeah, maybe I am."

Pastor Dale dumped a couple packets of sugar into his cup and stirred. "The reasoning being that if you don't tell her how you feel and you discover she doesn't reciprocate your feelings, your heart stays intact?"

That was the reasoning. But not the truth. His heart would be shattered. His consolation was that at least no one else would know.

Dale walked over to Trey, and their gazes locked. "But if you don't tell her you love her, she'll have no reason to stay. She'll go back to Fort Worth."

His friend's blunt appraisal rocked him. "I can't let her do that. I can't let her go. She's everything to me."

Dale clasped a hand on Trey's shoulder. "Then, my friend, I think you'd better lay aside your pride and fight for the girl." He gave him a warm smile of encouragement. "And for what it's worth, my money's on you."

Trey practically pounced on Mrs. Nichols in her Sunday school classroom while she and several other ladies waited for the teacher to arrive. "I've haven't seen Hallie. Do you know where she is?"

Mrs. Nichols shook her head and sighed. "She's gone. She left first thing this morning. She said she had to get back to her life."

His heart took a dive. Hallie was gone. He had his answer. A woman in love wouldn't tear out of town at first light.

"Oh. Okay. Thanks." His shoulders sagged. Heartbroken and defeated, he turned to go. History seemed to repeat itself. He'd thought she was settling in when, in reality, she couldn't wait to get out of his one-horse town.

Halfway to the door, he halted. What was he doing? Ten years ago, he'd let her go without a fight. Win or lose, he wouldn't let that happen again.

He straightened and hurried back to Mrs. Nichols's side. "Do you have her home address in Fort Worth?"

"As a matter of fact, I do." She lifted her handbag from the floor and set it on the table in front of her. "I keep an address book in here. You can't imagine how many times it has come in handy."

She unzipped the purse and slowly flipped through every single paper and item in the well-stocked bag. One. By. One. Several greeting cards, a pack of tissues, an old envelope with a list on it, a receipt from Grocery Giant . . . It was all he could do to restrain himself from snatching the purse from her hands and searching it himself.

"I know it's in here . . ."

Trey's heart beat in double time. Seconds ticked away. Each one put more distance between him and the woman he loved.

"Oh, here it is." She pulled a small, flowered book from the bag with a triumphant flourish.

He grabbed it from her waving hand. "Thank you." He was already flipping the pages. "I'll just get the information and give it right back to you."

He entered the address into his phone, his fingers uncharacteristically clumsy on the tiny keypad, and returned it to her. "Thanks so much."

He dashed out of the classroom, through the crowded fellowship hall, and out to his truck. His plans were still fuzzy at this point. No eloquent words waited on his tongue. He knew only that he had to find Hallie and convince her to stay.

Hallie didn't pass a single car while she drove slowly down Main Street, marveling again at the treasure they'd unearthed from beneath years of deterioration and neglect. The once boarded-up relic looked hopeful and, though her heart was weighted with grief, she was proud of her part in preparing Trey's home for a brighter future.

She blinked back tears, took a right at the flashing yellow light, and pulled out onto the highway. She never imagined leaving would be so hard.

Ten feet ahead, she saw the new sign.

She pulled off the highway onto the shoulder. Nearly blinded by tears, she read:

Now Leaving Village Green

The Place Where You Belong

She dropped her face into her hands and wept.

Trey sped down Main Street and squealed onto the highway. His eyes shot wide when he saw a car, Hallie's car, parked at the foot of the new city limits sign. Heart pounding, he swerved off the road and onto the gravel shoulder, killed the engine, and jumped out of the truck.

"Hallie!"

She lowered the window, keeping her face averted.

It all came down to this moment. He was scared to death. He had no idea what to say. *Show me, Lord.*

Semi-paralyzed with fear, he rested a hand on the roof of her car and leaned down. "So, what are you doing?"

Really? His entire future was on the line and that's the best he could do?

Her eyes still fixed straight ahead, she shrugged.

His heart crashed. She wouldn't even look at him. Black despair washed over him. Who did he think he was? He could never hold her here. Then he saw it. A single tear trailed down Hallie's smooth cheek. She swiped a forearm across her eyes and sniffled.

She was crying! Praise God!

He yanked open the door and pulled her from the car, into his arms. "Oh, Hallie."

He held her close, gathering her to his heart. "What's the matter, baby?"

"I don't want to go." Her muffled answer was half words, half tears.

"Good because I can't let you."

She pulled away and looked at him with dark, tear-drenched eyes. "Why?"

"Because I love you." He cradled her face in his hands, stroking his thumb over her cheek. "I love you, Hallie. You are everything to me, and I don't want to live without you."

Fresh tears spilled over her cheeks. "Really? You love me? I mean I hoped you could, but—" She frowned and narrowed her eyes. "You don't think you're just grateful to me, do you? Since I helped out with the town and all? I think it would be easy to confuse gratitude for love."

He shook his head. "No confusion here. I'm surer of my feelings for you than I've ever been of anything in my life. I love you. I've never loved any woman but you. And I want to spend the rest of my life with you."

"Oh, Trey, I love you." She fitted her hands over his. "I've never loved another man but you. And I will happily spend the rest of my life with you."

He lowered his mouth to hers and kissed her with every ounce of his being. He was so caught up in kissing her, he didn't notice the police car pull up in front of Hallie's car.

"Hey, you two," Sam called through his lowered window. "Is there a problem here?"

Trey straightened but didn't take his eyes off Hallie's face. "Not at all, officer. Hallie just saw the sign there and realized Village Green was the place where she belongs."

Hallie and Trey sat side by side on the old wooden swing on her mother's porch, Trey's arm a comfortable weight across her shoulders while they watched the sun slip below the horizon. All around them crickets sang, and a welcome breeze stirred the late spring air.

He traced lazy circles on her upper arm. "I like the idea of having the ceremony in the church, but what do you say to having the reception on the Green, at the gazebo?"

Hallie frowned. Though thoroughly secure in his love, she couldn't forget the painful associations of the gazebo in the past.

He caught her look. "What is it?" He leaned in, his expression tender. "Talk to me. Tell me, why don't you like the gazebo?"

She dropped her gaze. "The night we broke up you were walking over to my house, and I decided to surprise you and meet you halfway." She took a deep breath and turned slightly to look directly into his eyes. "When I got to the Green, I saw you kissing Janice in the gazebo."

He screwed up his face, a combination of genuine confusion, shock, and horror. "No way. I would never kiss Janice." He paused for a moment, as though searching for the lost memory. "Oh wait. You know, I think she might have kissed *me* that night."

She lifted a brow. "She kissed you, and you didn't remember?"

He shook his head. "No. It wasn't really a kiss. She just sorta threw herself at me and smashed her lips to mine. You remember how crazy she was back then. I figured she was pranking me or something. She knew I was in love with you." He stopped the gentle swaying of the porch swing and stared her. "Wait a minute. Are you telling me you walked away from me all those years ago because you thought I had a thing for Janice?"

Hallie lowered her eyes and nodded. "She was so beautiful . . ."

He caught her chin and tipped her face up to his. "No, Hallie. Not as beautiful as you. There has never been anyone for me but you." He bent and placed a soft kiss on her lips. "Man, when I think of all the time we've wasted because of the stupid gazebo, I wish we'd torn the thing down with the revitalization."

With the twenty-twenty vision of hindsight, Hallie was finally able to see clearly. The years weren't wasted. Even in the darkest moments, God was working. She laid her head on his shoulder and took his strong hand in hers. "I'm sorry about the lost time, but honestly, I think I needed those years to grow up. If I had stayed here, I don't know if I'd have ever changed." She straightened to look at him. "It doesn't matter now. I'm just glad that in the end, God brought me back here, back to you."

Smiling, he pulled her close and kissed her tenderly. "Back to the place where you belong."